DOWN THE GARDEN PATH

DOWN THE
GARDEN PATH

Gerald Hammond

This first world edition published in Great Britain 2003 by
SEVERN HOUSE PUBLISHERS LTD of
9–15 High Street, Sutton, Surrey SM1 1DF.
This first world edition published in the USA 2003 by
SEVERN HOUSE PUBLISHERS INC of
595 Madison Avenue, New York, N.Y. 10022.

British Library Cataloguing in Publication Data

Hammond, Gerald, 1926-
   Down the garden path
   1.   Gardeners - Fiction
   2.   Detective and mystery stories
   I.   Title
   823.9'14 [F]

   ISBN 0-7278-5951-X

Typeset by Hewer Text Ltd.,
Edinburgh, Scotland.
Printed and bound in Great Britain by
MPG Books Ltd., Bodmin, Cornwall.

I am obliged to Jim McColl, noted for *Beechgrove Garden* and for his writing in the *Press and Journal*. I consulted him about such gardening matters as I thought might concern the knowledgeable reader. Any errors remaining may be put down to my stupidity or to the eccentric gardening habits of my main character.

For once, I have been geographically fairly specific, so I must explain that Cannaluke Lodge is fictitious and that the unidentified nearby village is not Spinningdale. Although circumstances may point to a person who exists in the real world, I would like to state that all the characters are totally and absolutely as fictitious as I could make them.

    G.H.

One

It was not in May Forsyth's nature to make firm decisions. A few occasions in her youth when she had overcome a natural hesitation and her inherent shyness enough to behave decisively had each proved unfortunate, not to say disastrous. She had drifted passively through her years as a student, absorbing the knowledge that was thrust upon her and going in search of more enlightenment. However, on her emergence into the real world she had found that any progression up the ladder of promotion brought with it unwelcome responsibility, exposure and an obligation to make decisions on behalf of others and, worse, to order them around. Even when she was clear in her mind what had to be done, she often found it impossible to choose and seize the proper moment for doing it. And so her one major (and perhaps wise) decision had been to remain firmly near the bottom of the heap.

When couples, or whole families, came to view the big house, May had paid them no attention. Then, when the successful purchasers made another visit to look at the property with eyes made keener by acquisition, she knew where her duty lay but she shrank from accosting them to introduce herself. Instead, she manufactured reasons to hide in one of the greenhouses. No doubt in due course they would make contact with her. Over the local grapevine, usually so accurate, she gathered that Mr Wheatley had made his money in Edinburgh, by designing some highly specialized computer programs used extensively by big business, as well as other software. Mrs Wheatley remained a total mystery.

Even when a large furniture van, belonging to an Edinburgh firm, discharged its load into the house, she disdained to watch the contents being unloaded. This was a great disappointment to those locals who had hoped for a synopsis of the quality and style of the newcomers' chattels, when she made one of her rare visits to the Firthview Inn that evening for a half of shandy. Cannaluke Lodge, after all, was an important house. Not to be compared with nearby Skibo Castle, perhaps, but important nevertheless. The character of its owners bore heavily on the lives of its immediate neighbours.

'I'm concerned with the garden,' she told Margaret Ferrier, one of the few neighbours with whom she felt sufficiently at ease for a good gossip. 'And that's all I'm concerned with. The house is nothing to me. If they don't want to keep me on, there are others who will.' This was undeniable. The garden of Cannaluke Lodge figured in the tourist literature and in occasional magazine articles. Visits by gardening freaks were common during the tourist season and May received, on average, one job offer every second month. Loyalty to the previous owners and a devotion to the garden, for the development of which she had been largely responsible, had so far restrained her; but one word out of place, she told herself, and she would definitely, probably go.

It was because of this philosophy as much as her personal shyness that she barely glanced up when, on an afternoon two days later, a well-up-the-range Jaguar stopped at the front door. The door was opened, presumably by Mrs Macdonald the housekeeper, and two figures passed inside.

May occupied the gardener's cottage between the garage and the two big greenhouses, a small but attractive dwelling of old brick, now neatly roughcast, and more recent tiles. (There were indications that it had originally been thatched.) During her occupancy, May had contrived to make the cottage both comfortable and internally almost smart; and the tiny kitchen was well enough equipped for her to provide herself with breakfast and an evening meal. By long-standing arrangement, however, she took lunch next day with Mrs Macdonald in the kitchen of the Lodge.

The housekeeper was a dumpy little lady of uncertain age, enormous energy and an unusual talent for *haute cuisine*. She had white hair and a red face and hands. Only a trace of her original Dundee accent was detectable. Although not by nature a chatterbox, she was usually happy to exchange a few words with May, but, being temporarily without help in the house, she had been hard put to it to cope with last-minute preparations for the new owners while providing them with what she considered to be appropriate meals.

May was hastily provided with a scratch meal, but with the addition of a half-glass of an excellent wine which had been left in the bottle the previous evening. Mrs Macdonald paused for a moment to say, 'He seems very nice, but she's stuck-up.' She lowered her voice until it was totally inaudible, but May, lip-reading, managed to make out the words 'Toffee-nosed', before Mrs Macdonald bustled out of the room again.

May was in the large tool shed, cleaning and racking her tools, when what remained of the light dimmed as a figure looked in at the door. Mr Wheatley, to judge from his silhouette, was of medium height but heavily built with close-cropped hair and small ears. Emerging into the light, May saw that he had a prominent nose but a face which was otherwise modest, intelligent and not unfriendly. His trousers belonged to a town suit but he was informally dressed otherwise, in a shirt worn open at the neck and a loose sweater. He for his part saw a woman in her later twenties who was small but obviously muscular, any tendency to plumpness in a well-shaped figure being kept well in check by physical work. He saw also dark curls springing in all directions, a round face disguised by horn-rimmed spectacles, well-worn jeans and a jumper which had suffered for some years from the attention of thorns.

Mr Wheatley hesitated. He bent and patted Ellery, May's spaniel, which put him immediately into the good books. She guessed that he was uncertain how to greet a female employee. To ease his way she said, 'How do you do? I'm May Forsyth, the gardener.'

He nodded, put out his hand and withdrew it again when she held hers up to let him see that they were well caked with earth. (For some jobs, gloves were essential; but in general May liked to be able to feel the texture and humidity of the soil.) 'I'm Grant Wheatley,' he said. 'The new owner. I may as well say that it's a lovely old house but it was the garden that really caught and held our fancy. I understand that you keep it all yourself?'

May shook her head, further disarranging her curls. An attempt to restore a little order resulted only in a smear of earth across her forehead. The time to set him straight had arrived of its own accord. 'Not entirely. I've often had at least one Work Experience youth to help me, sometimes more, and I can call on the garden centre when there's too much to cope with. Of course, you're seeing it at one of the best times of the year, but I try to keep it colourful all the year round. If it doesn't flower or fruit or berry, I don't want it. I've been interplanting the old laurels under the boundary trees with rhododendrons and azaleas. When they're established, the laurels can go. I take it that you agree?'

'Suppose I didn't?'

May decided that a life of contention would be more than she could face. 'Then I'd go and work for somebody else.'

He nodded and smiled. 'I'd heard that you could be a strong-minded young woman when your plans for the garden were in discussion. I prefer it that way. They say that the camel was a horse designed by a committee and I don't want a camel for my garden. This garden isn't just colourful. It looks natural and yet the colours seem to be . . . designed.'

'They are. I have a chart.' She gestured vaguely towards the door.

'May I see?' His voice was almost accentless.

Returning into the shed she was surprised to notice how quickly the light was fading. She switched on the lamps. On the wall beside the door was a large square of cartridge paper divided into a great many small rectangles. At first glance it seemed to be a hideous hodgepodge of random colour. Then he saw that the names of plants by the dozen, mostly in Latin and unfamiliar to him, were written neatly down the left-hand margin and the months of the year across the top. On a shelf below there was a fat swatch of much-cut-up paint-colour samples, a pair of scissors and a tube of glue.

'I'm still building it up,' she said, 'but if I want to remind myself what will be in flower at a particular time of the year and what will harmonize with it, I can refer to this.'

He was impressed and quite prepared to let her know it. 'That's amazingly methodical. But I approve. Whatever you set out to do, you should do as well as you possibly can. And I see that you're very well equipped.' He looked around. The large shed held a substantial sit-on lawnmower, a rotovator, a chainsaw and a strimmer, all petrol-driven, along with a large collection of lesser tools. He could see at a glance that all were very well kept.

'Mr Mellor, while he was alive, never grudged the cost of good tools,' May said. 'He thought that it came out cheaper than hiring extra labour. Some of the tools came from the garden centre, partly in exchange for plants that I raised in the greenhouses. I suppose that you bought the tools along with the house?'

'I believe I did, although I didn't pay attention to what I was getting. The list didn't look as impressive as the reality.' His interest had sharpened at the mention of the business aspect. He looked at her again. She was very well spoken and clearly was out of a different drawer from an everyday gardener. 'I see that you have a lot to tell me. Would you come up to the house later? Eightish? I don't think that a drink would be out of order.'

May suppressed a sigh. She had been looking forward to an hour or two in front of the telly or with a book before an early night. But a new employer had some rights. Not a lot, but some.

Promptly at eight, May walked wearily up to the house. Darkness was almost complete but she knew her path through the stable yard from long habit and could picture the house in front of her, a charming old house built of the local stone, with tall, twelve-paned windows. It had begun life as a large farmhouse and had been extended without any resort to the Victorian love of turrets and crow-steps. The result was a low and irregular but gracious building which visitors thought charming without quite knowing why. Even without the guidance of the lit windows, May could have found her way to the knocker of the kitchen door. During the day, she would have walked in, but this was a more formal occasion.

The door was opened by Gloria Penn, a local girl. Evidently, the process of engaging new staff had already begun. Gloria seemed uncertain whether to treat May, who had been the daughter of the local doctor, as a visitor or as a fellow member of staff. May had taught her to ride a bicycle but had later slapped her bottom, hard, for being cheeky. Gloria compromised by sketching the tentative beginning of a curtsey and then inviting May, by a jerk of the head, to follow her.

At the drawing-room door, Gloria knocked – a minor breach of etiquette, May noticed – and avoided any need to decide how to announce the visitor by omitting it altogether and allowing May to pass inside.

The house had always been maintained to a high standard and any modernizations, such as the central heating, had been incorporated with tact so that the room retained the gracious charm which May remembered. The Wheatleys had bought the carpets and curtains with the house, but the cretonne-covered antique chairs and settee, the occasional tables and upright tapestry chairs, had gone. The room looked bare, the floor occupied only by a large and luxurious suite covered in pale leather, several spindly side tables and a large television set. The sporting prints had also vanished from the walls, leaving pale squares on the flock wallpaper.

May's anomalous position in the local hierarchy was still making itself felt. She had taken a quick bath while her TV meal heated, then arranged her hair and, deciding against dressing down for the occasion, had donned her one remaining passable frock, battered her hair into submission and discarded her glasses. Her sudden appearance in the guise of a presentable young woman instead of a mud-stained gardener seemed to confuse her new employer, who hesitated, half rose and then got up from one of the easy chairs and offered it to May. 'This is my wife, Pauline, as you've probably guessed. Polly, this is Miss Forsyth. Would you care for a drink?' he asked May.

May thrust aside any feeling of awkwardness and sank gratefully into the deep chair. 'I'm more than ready for a gin and tonic, thank you,' she said. She wondered whether to add 'Sir', but there was going to be no forelock-tugging in the relationship.

Mrs Wheatley, who was seated in the other easy chair and sipping something green with ice, acknowledged the introduction with a nod. May guessed that she was not pleased to find the gardener seated in her presence but lacked the self-assurance to say so. May was not unsympathetic. She had had to teach herself to present a bold face to the world and could still easily become tongue-tied and graceless whenever she felt herself to be out of her element. Mrs Wheatley was of about her own build with a babyish face slightly past its first youth and golden hair which, May judged, owed only a little of its colour to the art of the hairdresser. Her dress, May thought, might have been suitable for receiving urban visitors but not for a quiet evening at home in the country.

Mr Wheatley put May's gin and tonic beside her, care-fully on a coaster, and carried his own whisky to the settee. 'Would you like to tell us a little about yourself?' he asked.

On the death of May's father, her invalid mother had found herself with just enough money to continue in the modest family home with a companion-cum-carer to look after her. May had found that sharing the house with an elderly invalid and her fussy companion was no sort of a life and had made her escape as soon as she could, but that would be of no concern, and probably of no interest, to the Wheatleys. 'About three years ago,' she said, 'the Mellors found themselves without a gardener. I had been advising them about the general design of the garden. It was originally very formal – copied from Dunrobin Castle, I think, which itself was modelled on Versailles – all very Inigo Jones rather than Capability Brown – and I did the original sketch, which had been pretty much adhered to, on the back of an envelope. So I agreed to help them, on a temporary basis, and it became permanent. The garden was well kept, at that time, but the planting was not very imaginative. I've spent my time getting it the way I think it should be. Then Mr Mellor died, as you must know. Mrs Mellor stayed on, but the house was much too big for her and in the end she decided to sell up.'

'It seems a lot of garden to be kept by one person,' Mrs Wheatley said doubtfully.

'It is,' May agreed.

'How have you managed?'

'Firstly, as I told Mr Wheatley, I've usually had one or two Work Experience boys to help. I hope you'll agree to continuing the arrangement?'

'Yes, certainly,' Mr Wheatley said. 'Just give us warn-ing.'

May began counting off the points on her fingers. 'Secondly, one of those boys now works for a local horticultural firm and I borrow him back once a week in summer to cut the grass. It doesn't cost much,' she added pacifically, 'because he's still only an apprentice. Thirdly, Mr Mellor let me call in the same horticultural firm when there was something major to be done. Fourthly, Mrs Mellor used to help me a lot in the garden. Fifthly, I've been trying to arrange everything in a labour-saving way. Shrubs with thick ground cover beneath and bulbs coming through, that sort of thing.'

Mr Wheatley was smiling. 'And sixthly?'

'If there's a sixthly,' May said, 'it's just that I've had to keep thinking time and motion. You know what I mean? You go from here to there to there instead of here and back and there and back. It's become a habit to think out the next moves while I carry out some manual task.'

'And working long hours, from what I hear,' he said. 'And never taking holidays except to visit other gardens.'

'I enjoy what I do,' May said simply.

'And what were you enjoying doing this afternoon beyond these windows?' Mrs Wheatley asked.

May glanced involuntarily at the windows. The curtains were closed but she could visualize the bed forty paces away with the single young conifer in it. 'Mostly, I was lifting the *vinca major*. Periwinkle,' she explained quickly. 'I want it for somewhere else and it doesn't thrive in such direct sunshine. Also, it would have been in the way when I take that tree out. The tree's in quite the wrong place. I have boxes of pansy seedlings ready to fill the gap.'

'You had a dog with you,' Mrs Wheatley said.

'She knows better than to pee on the lawn,' May said stiffly. 'Do you mind? I'm used to having her with me.

10

Sometimes I'm alone in a remote corner of the garden for ages.'

'I like that tree,' Mrs Wheatley said flatly.

'I can't believe that you know what it is,' said May.

Mr Wheatley was quick to break what might have been a tense silence. 'What brought you into gardening in the first place?' he asked.

'I have a degree in botanical sciences and I took a postgraduate course in landscape architecture.'

'From?'

'Cambridge. But I didn't enjoy any of the posts that were open to me, so I was happy to help the Mellors out.'

'I want that tree left where it is,' Mrs Wheatley said defiantly.

May finished her drink and put the glass down carefully on the coaster. 'If you prefer to find somebody else,' she said, 'I would quite understand. Thank you for the drink.' She rose, wished her hosts a good night and walked stiffly out of the room.

Mr Wheatley followed her into the hall. 'Just a minute,' he said. 'There's no question of wanting anyone else. But what's wrong with that tree?'

'It's a *sequoia sempervirens*,' May said. 'The giant redwood. It grows quickly to a hundred feet tall in Britain and three times that in America. I didn't even realize what it was myself until I noticed from my photographs how it was shooting up. I don't know what Joe Scott was thinking of. Probably Mrs Mellor brought it home without realizing what it was and Joe could be a malicious devil at times. If he was in a bad mood at the time, he might just have planted it and waited to see what would happen when it went on growing.'

Her new employer nodded and smiled. 'Let's get rid of

11

it, by all means,' he said. 'And, please, no more talk about finding somebody else. I'm sure that nobody else would put as much expertise and – yes – love into the place.'

May returned to her cottage, much mollified but not looking forward to her next encounter with Mrs Wheatley.

Two

T he next day dawned fine and clear. May wasted no more than a minute or two in enjoying the prospect of the garden. The grass was returning to its spring-time green. It had been laid out unbroken for easy mowing, but the wide lawn in front of the house led off into grassy pathways between beds in which the verges of flowering ground cover rose into shrubs and then to central specimen trees. The rising ground beside the house was broken into terraces by drystone walls where flowers tumbled.

The garden sloped south towards a strip of water garden and the Dornoch Firth. The view in that direction was spectacular, across the firth. Farms mingling with woodland rose to meet the hills of Easter Ross. The snow had gone from the hills but one mountaintop, still with snow in the corries, peeked over the hills. (Was it *Carn Bhren* or *Beinn Clach An Fheadain*? She really must find out some day.) The other boundaries were screened by strips of woodland and by the laurels which were soon to be superseded by rhododendrons and azaleas.

May spent a valuable hour dividing up clumps of delphiniums and replanting them where she wanted a blaze of their unique blue through the later summer. Duke Ellon had arrived to cut the grass and she saw him established with the mower and made sure that he remembered just how she liked the mowings disposed of for compost. Then it was into the cooler of the greenhouses, where later Mrs Wheatley found her.

Pauline Wheatley had reverted to a simple cotton dress which, May thought, was better suited both to her and to the occasion. May cringed inwardly, wondering whether she was to face another exhibition of cold hostility.

Mrs Wheatley seemed ill at ease but her manner was not hostile. 'Hullo,' she said. 'What are you doing?'

May thought that what she was doing was fairly obvious but she remained polite. 'These seedlings are ready to pot up,' she said.

'And who's this?'

'This' was Ellery, May's spaniel. May introduced her.

'What sort is he?'

'She. The breed's Welsh springer. You can always tell them. English springers are liver and white or black and white but Welsh are red and white.'

Mrs Wheatley absorbed the information and stooped to give the springer a pat. 'Can I help?' she asked.

The cotton dress would take no harm. May cast around for a foolproof task. 'You could fill these pots from this barrow for me.' May demonstrated the placing of broken crocks in the bottom of each pot.

Mrs Wheatley ran her fingers doubtfully through the potting compost. 'What is this stuff?'

'My own mixture. Loam, peat and sand.' May decided not to mention the well-rotted manure.

The two women worked in harmony for a few minutes.

'I suppose you thought I was daft last night,' Mrs Wheatley said suddenly.

May had already recognized the abruptness which can come from acute shyness because she was sometimes guilty

of it herself. 'Not really. You said you liked the tree where
it was, which was fair comment. You didn't know that it
was going to tower over the house. I just thought that you
didn't have much experience of gardening.'

'That's true. Nor of a country house and . . . and staff
and things.' The confession came out in a gust of relief.
'We had a flat. Grant had to come here for a court case
and he had nothing to do in his evenings except drive
around. He just loved the countryside here and when he
saw this house and garden with the agent's sign saying that
it was for sale there was no holding him. Well, I had my
doubts. I was only too happy to have him retire instead of
working himself into a heart attack. It's beautiful here. But
I don't know anybody,' she finished plaintively.

'Nobody at all?'

'Almost nobody. Grant met one or two people while he
was here.'

May's dislike of her new employer's wife had melted
completely. She could understand only too well the bad
impression that shy people can make. 'I don't think people
leave cards much any more,' she said helpfully. 'What you
should do is to give a cocktail party, or even better a dinner
party, for the people your husband knows, for them to
meet each other. Then they invite you in return to meet
others that they know and so it goes on. Mrs Macdonald
knows all about dinner parties, she'll keep you straight.'

Mrs Wheatley turned out to have the knack of transferring the tiny plants from box to pot without disturbing a
single root fibre. When the whole batch was finished, she
looked around tidy ranks in the greenhouse. 'My God!' she
said. 'We'll never get to use this many flowers. Or will we?'

May hid a smile. 'What we've been doing just now were
brassicas. Vegetables,' she explained. 'To fill in gaps in

your vegetable garden, behind those high walls, as we pull veggies for the table. Most of the rest are flowers. The garden centre sells any surplus for me, or we take an exchange for whatever we need at the time. It's only sense really. It takes only seconds to pop a few seeds into a box or cuttings into a pot and then you forget about it for a while and suddenly you've got a whole lot of valuable plants.'

'I'll be damned!' Mrs Wheatley seemed much struck by this exposition. She smiled suddenly, transforming her face. 'I bet it isn't as simple as that. I'll have to go soon. I'll think about what you've said. But I feel better already. I do know somebody now. You.'

Ellery preceded her to the greenhouse door and offered her a paw to shake.

For all her friendly words, it was a week before Pauline Wheatley visited May again. The day was cool and damp and May was taking advantage of suitable weather to plant out some Bouvardia against a low wall where they would be seen from the window of the dining room.

Mrs Wheatley came out through the French windows and approached. Ellery bounced towards her and rolled over to have her underside patted.

'What are we planting out this time?'

'I've nearly finished,' May said. 'And there's only one kneeler. But you can finish off while I fetch water, if you like. It's winter jasmine, all from cuttings taken last year off two old shrubs that I found beside the summerhouse. They'll give you an extra touch of colour in winter.'

'I'm all for that.'

When May returned with two large watering cans, the last plants were in place. They set about watering them in.

'Now that you've told me about it,' Mrs Wheatley said, 'I've taken against that tree. I can imagine it towering over the house and blotting out the sky. And the view. When are you taking it down?'

'I'm waiting for the farmer to come and help me,' May said. 'But he keeps saying that he's too busy.'

Several days later, May noticed that Duke Ellon had again forgotten her instructions and dumped the grass mowings in an undiluted pile on the compost heap, where they would soon settle into a slimy and valueless lump. She was energetically turning the pile and mixing in the previous autumn's leaves and some strips of newspaper when Pauline Wheatley sought her out. May greeted her with a smile. She had come to like the other woman – an alliance of the socially maladroit.

'We did just as you suggested. A dinner party.'

May was happy to rest her back for a minute by leaning on her fork. Obviously, there was more to come. 'And?'

'And just as you said, Mrs Macdonald knew exactly what we should do, even to recommending a man from the Mitre Hotel to come and be butler.'

'Mr Henson, I expect,' May said. 'He does it for most of the hostesses. He'll keep you straight about wines and suchlike if you're not too sure. He was butler in one of the stately homes until his lordship went bust. Tell me when it is and I'll make sure that there are flowers for the table.'

'It's tomorrow night.' Mrs Wheatley made a gesture as though brushing away an irritating fly. 'But that isn't what's bothering me. We've got two couples coming and another man who Grant met while he was here. Grant didn't know much about him but sort of assumed that he had a wife somewhere, or at least a partner, but now it seems he's a widower and it means that I'm a girl short.'

'And you want me to suggest a few candidates for a blind date?' May straightened up and began a mental review of eligible single ladies.

Mrs Wheatley's agitation increased. 'No, it's not that. I want to ask you to come. Grant said not to—'

May nodded sagely. 'He's right, of course. It isn't exactly *de rigueur* to invite your gardener to the dinner table.'

The other lady, now that her attitude had suffered a complete *volte-face*, looked shocked at the suggestion of such snobbery. 'He didn't mean that either. He just said that if you clicked with the guest, we'd never be able to find such a good gardener again.'

May leaned on her fork and laughed until the tears came. 'Thank him from me,' she said. 'That's a compliment and a half. I'll have to get it carved somewhere.'

Polly Wheatley joined in the laughter. She had a deep, snorting laugh which May thought was funnier than the joke. 'Looking at it that way, I think it's two complete compliments,' Polly said.

May sobered suddenly. 'But you'll be dressing up and I don't have a thing to wear,' she said. 'And that's not just the old excuse. Anything I have is hopelessly dated and all this physical work has changed my shape quite a lot. And – forgive my mentioning it – gardeners' wages don't run to *haute couture*. Don't think I'm complaining,' she added hastily as the other's face fell. 'I love my work and I wouldn't expect special treatment, but the local boutique's beyond my means and you wouldn't want me lowering the tone at your dinner table.'

Mrs Wheatley's hands moved in an agitated gesture.

'But that's no problem. We're pretty much the same size. I
can lend you something. Come up to the house this
evening and we'll try things on. Please do say yes. I want
you there.' She flushed. 'I'm not used to giving dinner
parties, just carry-out suppers with people eating on their
knees and passing bottles around. You'll be able to give me
a frown if I'm going to use the wrong fork or something.'

The invitation was evidently heartfelt and May was not
averse to eating one of Mrs Macdonald's best dinners, but
she was cautious. 'Who's coming?' she asked.

'The single man is some sort of business contact of
Grant's from Inverness, and so's the man half of one of
the couples. I've never met either of them. The single man's
name is Largs and the couple is Welles and that's all I
know about them. And there's a Mr and Mrs Heatherton
from Spinningdale. Grant and I decided to walk down to
the firth and along to the village that way and we met them
when we were on the way back. We went with them for
coffee at the pub and we seemed to get along – they were
really charming and I think they liked us – so I invited
them. I hope they're OK. Do you know them?'

'They're my aunt and uncle. That's all right then. I'd
love to come.'

May had intended to make one of her visits to the pub that
evening, but Mrs Wheatley's invitation promised to be
more useful and more interesting. She put on her one
almost passable dress again and, deciding that she was
there as a guest, she presented herself at the front door of
the house and was admitted by Mrs Wheatley herself.

'I saw you coming up the path. I was watching for you.'

The two statements seemed to call for no answer. May
followed her hostess up a surprisingly narrow oak stair to

an upper hallway where doorways and passages led off at unexpected angles. Mrs Wheatley led the way into what was the master bedroom. A large waterbed looked remarkably out of place against the linenfold panelling.

Mrs Wheatley opened a smaller door to a big, walk-in closet. This was hung with enough clothes to stock a small boutique. It was evident that the age of prosperity for the Wheatleys had not dawned very recently, because May could recognize some very expensive fabrics and designer labels. She could see at a glance that most of the dresses were altogether too fancy to be worn at an informal dinner in the country – especially by an off-duty gardener, she added wryly to herself. Additionally, it seemed that the few formal dresses were strapless, rendering them less suitable for her smaller bust, and the colours had been chosen to set off a blonde rather than a dark brunette.

Half an hour spent holding one garment after another against herself and studying the effect in a standing mirror confirmed that impression. 'They're not exactly me, are they?' she said. 'I'd better just wear this old thing.'

'The red velvet wasn't too bad.'

May tried it again. It might do at a pinch but . . . 'Mrs Wheatley—'

The other woman had seated herself on a stool by an ornate dressing table. 'Please, call me Polly,' she broke in. She sounded flustered. 'I mean, look, you're not the ordinary run of gardeners and I don't have any friends around here. I don't really miss the ones I left behind, there wasn't one of them I'd trust not to run me down behind my back, but I'd like to have somebody to talk to, somebody who'd call me by my first name. And I want to fit in here but I don't know about country ways and you do.'

May saw that she had turned pink and showed all the

signs of acute embarrassment. She joined the other on the window seat. 'Polly, then,' May said. 'Call me May and ask me anything you don't know, any time. But I really wouldn't be comfortable queening it in red velvet at your dinner table.'

'Well, then, May.' Polly Wheatley seemed to be more at ease now that a first-name relationship had been established. 'Here's another suggestion. There's a trunk in the attic. It was left in the room we wanted for best spare room. I looked inside and it's mostly dresses. They'd been carefully packed but left behind. I thought it had been left by mistake so I phoned Mrs Mellor.

'She choked up. She rang off and had to call me back much later. She said that the staff had packed the clothes but she never wanted to see them again and to give them to Oxfam or something. Well, they didn't seem to be the sort of thing the Bosnian or Afghan peasants would wear around the fields, so I had our removers put the trunk up in the attic for me while I looked for the name of a shop that would sell them for charity. What was it all about, do you suppose?'

'I can look out a phone number for you,' May said. 'Mrs Mellor had a daughter who ran off with somebody totally unsuitable. They were terribly upset at the time. That's whose it'll be. Mrs Mellor's a rather emotional woman. I can well imagine her not being able to face going into Janet's room after she left and not wanting to see her clothes again. Janet's younger than I am, but much the same size and shape and closer to my colour than you are, so I don't see any harm taking a look.'

They took a look. The attic was remarkably dust-free, considering the age of the house. May thought that Mrs Macdonald could have been counted on not to waste her time while the house was otherwise empty.

A large, brass-bound trunk was centrally placed and it did indeed contain dresses and other clothes. May drew out a dress of dark-blue polyester printed with a faint pattern, which seemed to strike the right balance between smartness and the modesty befitting a gardener.

'If it fits, I'll keep it and give the charity shop a donation,' May said.

Back in the bedroom, she tried it on. The fitting was a success, except that Mr Wheatley walked in while May was between dresses. He apologized quickly, saying that he had heard them leave the bedroom and thought that they had finished. But he winked at May as he withdrew.

The following evening May checked in the mirror one last time and decided that the blue dress, as she had thought, was neither too modest nor too flamboyant and the paucity of jewellery was quite appropriate. She had a pair of leather slippers which were almost a match. It had been some time since she had visited a hairdresser but her hair, which spent most days blowing free or tied back in a ponytail, had brushed out into satisfactory waves. Her hands had needed more attention than all the rest of her but they would pass in a dim light and at least her nails were clean. She was looking, if not her absolute best, quite good enough to be the emergency blind date for a spare dinner guest.

Although quite capable of chatting at length to a close friend about any subject which caught her interest, she had never had confidence in her conversational abilities. Rather than risk having to stumble indefinitely through a morass of small talk, she deliberately waited at an open window until she had heard the quiet purr of her uncle's Rover and the rasp of a heavier vehicle. Before she set off for the house, she lingered until intuition told her that the gathering would have got beyond the first embarrassing hiatus, first warning Ellery to stay in and behave herself. A large, American-built four-by-four stood beside her uncle's car outside the front door. The Canarybird climbing rose on the front wall was in full bloom but she lifted a leaf to check for greenfly.

The portly Mr Henson, definitely ageing but still dignified, brought her to the drawing room and furnished her with a champagne cocktail. Conversation was already general. The men, as she had expected, were wearing dinner jackets. She was greeted politely by Mr Wheatley and with relief by Polly. She pecked her aunt and uncle on one cheek apiece and shook hands with Bob Welles, a sandy-haired man with an excitingly resonant voice, nice-looking apart from a once broken nose, and with his wife, Jenny.

The other man, introduced to her as Will Largs, was tough looking, with a very square jaw, black hair and shaggy eyebrows. Heavily built, he was putting on additional weight and his dinner jacket had been acquired when he was comparatively slim. Her slight astigmatism and the lack of her spectacles rendered him slightly blurred, which she thought probably suited him, but she could see that his mouth had prominent, well-defined lips and a curl which she took to be supercilious. He carried with him an air of power and intolerance which in other surroundings would have intimidated her. She was immediately visited by a sense of *déjà vu*.

With such a small company there was no need to split into small groups, but she had been invited to partner him so she addressed him with some trivial comment about the weather. As soon as she heard his voice, memory made the connection. 'Haven't we met somewhere before?' she asked him.

He produced a smile which redeemed his face. 'It seems unlikely,' he said, in a deep voice quite devoid of the soft, Highland accent. 'But then, I meet an awful lot of people. Or a lot of awful people, whichever way you like to look at it.'

Either the smile or his voice, or perhaps some turn of phrase triggered a sudden recollection. 'It was at the garden centre, the big one in Dingwall.' He looked at her blankly and she remembered that she would have been wearing jeans or corduroys and her hair would probably have been tied back under an old hat of either felt or straw, depending on the weather. She would almost certainly have had her heavy glasses on, although on occasions, such as this evening, she could easily manage without them. 'You were buying a camellia,' she reminded him.

He raised a finger but restrained himself from pointing at her. His smile, when it came back, turned his expression from daunting to warm and friendly. 'And you told me to plant it where it wouldn't see the sun at least until afternoon. I don't think that I thanked you properly at the time, but you were quite right. It's thriving where it is.'

'I'm glad. Putting a plant in the wrong place always seems as cruel as taking an animal out of its natural habitat.'

He chuckled. He seemed to be giving careful consideration to a reply when Mr Henson announced dinner. He crooked his arm, she laid two fingers on it and they went through.

In the dining room, the carpet and curtains had again been sold with the house as being impossibly unsuited to

Mrs Mellor's new and much smaller abode. White cloths almost obscured the fact that two smaller tables had replaced the original. The chairs were good reproductions which May guessed had been an emergency purchase. May could remember occasions when the Mellors had entertained upwards of twenty guests, but the table managed to look well by candlelight and with the flowers that she had cut and arranged that afternoon, flaunting themselves in a silver bowl.

May was seated on Grant Wheatley's left with her aunt opposite. They had begun on the melon *hors d'oeuvre* and Mr Henson was pouring wine when Mrs Heatherton looked more closely at her niece. 'That's a pretty dress,' she said. 'I don't think I've seen it before. Or have I?'

'Possibly,' May said, 'but not on me. I didn't have anything suitable. Mrs Wheatley kindly offered to lend me a dress but hers were all a little too dressy for me.' (The company all glanced at Polly Wheatley, who was looking sumptuous in the red dress that May had considered. May had been pleased to note that her hostess had taken her advice and made only restrained use of her jewellery.) 'Then,' May resumed, 'she remembered that Mrs Mellor had left a trunk behind. I presume that the clothes in it belonged to Janet, the daughter who eloped. This was in it. Mrs Mellor said to give the clothes to Oxfam. I may decide to keep this and make Oxfam a donation, because I think it suits me and if I'm lucky the Wheatleys may go on holding me as a reserve for whenever they have a spare male coming to dinner.'

'Not as a reserve but a member of the team. I thought you were going to call me Polly,' her hostess said reproachfully.

'Not in company,' May said. 'I'm an employee.'

'Of course!' Mrs Wheatley paused and frowned uncertainly. 'Oh, was that clumsy of me?'

'Not at all,' May said. 'It's what I am.'

'And a damned good one too,' Grant Wheatley said stoutly. 'You should all see the garden by daylight.'

'There's a testimonial for you,' May's uncle said. 'But we have seen it in daytime. We knew Mrs Mellor quite well. I used to do business with her husband.'

'My dear,' said her aunt to May, 'your grandmother, who was a real stickler, would have approved of your meticulousness – if there is such a word – but I think that, on a social occasion and after being invited, you could use Polly's first name.'

'There!' Polly said triumphantly.

A girl from the village came in to serve the soup. May had seen her around although she could not put a name to her. The girl was very neat in black with a frilled apron – undoubtedly Mrs Macdonald's view of the formality proper in a gentleman's house. When that distraction was past, Mr Largs, from May's left, asked her, 'But how do you come to be a gardener? You don't seem to fit the part.'

'She has a degree,' Mr Wheatley said.

May looked up from buttering a roll. 'I have a degree in horticulture,' she confirmed placidly, 'and a diploma in landscape architecture, but I found that all I could do with them was teach children or go into some research establishment.

'I tried them both and hated them. I was staying at home, only a few miles away, doing minor gardening jobs for friends and wondering what to do with my life, when Mrs Mellor told me that Joe Scott, who was the gardener here, had run off. The garden was threatening to go back to the Indians and she asked me would I please come and do what I could until they could get a replacement gardener. I was very fond of them both and I'd already helped them to design the garden, because Joe, despite being very competent at nurturing plants and pruning and so on, had no more idea about garden design than fly in the air. Also, I was sorry for them, they'd had a lot of sadness, so I came to help them out. We got on very well and I loved the job, so I moved into the gardener's cottage and I've been working very happily here ever since.'

'And long may it continue,' Grant Wheatley said.

'The sadness you referred to,' Mr Largs said. 'Was that the daughter running off?'

'Janet,' May said. 'There had been a son, older than Janet, who'd drowned off a yacht in the Mediterranean some years earlier. It seemed to knock the stuffing out of both of them and Janet running off was almost the last straw. And Mr Mellor had already had his first heart attack. His heart killed him not long after Janet vanished. Mrs Mellor stayed on for a couple of years, but the house was much too large for her and it wasn't the same with only herself and the servants. I think the combined memories of the boy – Bruce – and her husband and Janet were too strong for her.'

'Did the daughter run off with the gardener, or was that coincidence?' Mr Largs asked.

'I don't think it was even much of a coincidence,' said Mrs Heatherton. 'They went in the same year, but they were very different people and Janet went first, by some weeks as I remember. There had been some word of a boyfriend. Then Scott, who had always been a terror for the women despite having a wife somewhere, disappeared and there was a lot of local speculation as to whether he'd debunked with one of them or been chased away by an angry husband.'

27

'He was a good enough gardener, I believe,' said May's uncle, 'but I don't think anyone was sorry to see the back of him.'

The wine went round again. Only Jenny Welles refused another glass on the grounds that she had to drive.

'Good Lord!' May said. 'Are you driving that monster?'

Mrs Welles made a face and put out the tip of her tongue at her husband. She was an attractive young woman with vivid colouring, black hair cut short, and an expression of lively interest. 'If I don't agree to drive them,' she said, 'those two refuse the invitation and I don't get taken anywhere. Actually, it's not as bad to drive as you'd think. It has automatic gears and power everything. I don't mind doing a country run. Just don't ask me to park it in a city street. I imagine that taking a liner into dry dock must be much the same.'

'I never did manage to reach any such sensible arrangement,' May's uncle said.

'I gave up driving years ago,' said her aunt. 'The good Henson came for us. He left his own car and drove us over in ours. That means that we can let our hair down.' Grant Wheatley took the hint and nodded to Mr Henson, who plied the bottle again.

Conversation wandered far afield and did not return to gardening until the iced ginger mousse had been served. By then, Mr Largs had invited her to call him William or just Will. She had gained a first impression that he was rather humourless, but when, encouraged by the wine, she ventured a slightly obscure joke which passed over the other heads she happened to be turned towards him and they shared a momentary glance of amusement. 'In exchange for a dinner out almost as good as this one,' he said, 'would you come and look at my roses some time? I do all right with floribundas and hybrid teas, but my rambler roses are a mess.'

May was uncertain whether or not there was a faint suggestion of etchings in the background. She was warming to him despite his rather forbidding appearance, but she was accepting no invitations in her slightly tipsy state. It was a pity to miss out on a good dinner, but the probable solution to his problem was already evident. 'When do you prune them?' she asked.

'Same time as the others.'

'And the same way?'

'Yes.'

'There's your problem. Ramblers flower next year on the stems that didn't flower this year. Prune them as soon as they've finished flowering and take out only the shoots that have just flowered and Bob may very well turn out to be your uncle.'

Polly Wheatley, who was undoubtedly feeling the effects of the wine, broke in on Mr Largs's thanks. 'I see the giant redwood's still out there,' she said, nodding towards the curtained windows. 'I swear it's grown another foot or two since we spoke about it.'

'It's probably grown six inches while we've been sitting here. I have a problem,' said May. 'I usually get the farmer to bring a tractor to pull down trees but he says he can't spare it for the moment. I've already done some digging around the roots to loosen them.'

'Why don't you just cut it down?' Grant Wheatley asked.

'Because if I do that, the stump will be in the way for years and suckers and fungus will keep coming up through the grass from all the roots. One good pull would fetch it out, roots and all. Then I thought we might plant a lilac instead, or maybe a laburnum. There's one behind the kitchen garden but I think it's already too big to transplant. No, I've got it.' She made a delighted gesture which nearly knocked over her glass. 'A *viburnum opulus sterile*. The snowball tree. With a clematis climbing up it. I'll phone the farmer again in the morning. Or,' she craned her neck in the direction of Jenny Welles, 'would that big beast of yours shift it?'

'Not mine,' Jenny said.

'Mine,' Will Largs said. 'Some of the places I have to go, I need it. I haven't seen many things it won't pull. I dragged a lorry out of a ditch last winter. How big is the tree?'

'About twenty feet,' Grant Wheatley said. 'Perhaps more. You can see it from the window.'

Will got up and looked between the curtains. There was a brilliant moon. 'Dead easy,' he said, returning to his seat. 'Conifers aren't deep-rooted and you've already loosened the roots. If you have a rope?'

'I have a good nylon rope,' said May. 'Mr Mellor brought it home when we were pulling out the alders where the water garden is now. When could you come back and do it?'

'We live near Inverness, more than forty miles off. Let's do it now.' He began to rise.

'There's still cheese to come,' Grant Wheatley protested. 'And coffee and liqueurs. And cigars for those who like them.'

Largs subsided reluctantly.

May was not going to let the chance go by. She was feeling a little light-headed and decidedly adventurous and she already seemed to have talked more that evening than in the previous year. 'I don't feel like coffee,' she said.

'Thank you for my lovely dinner. I'll go and get that rope. The gentlemen can bring their cigars outside. Mrs Mellor never would allow cigars to be smoked in the dining room. She said it rotted the wallpaper or something. Excuse me.'

She left the room, walking with less than her usual precision.

'You'd better change that dress,' her aunt called after her.

Three

A few years earlier, her aunt's words would have switched May into a rebellious mode. But now, she told herself firmly, she was her own woman, no longer subject to the edicts of fussy elders. She could change the dress or not, just as she pleased. She could go for a swim in it or tear it up for floor cloths, if she so wished. By the time she had reached her own door, she had realized that the deciding factor was her promise to send a donation to charity if she kept the dress.

Entering, to an ecstatic welcome from Ellery, who had, as usual, been quite certain that she had been deserted for ever, May hurried to the bedroom and removed the dress, draping it carefully over the one chair. While she hunted for the jeans and jumper that she had removed only a few hours earlier, she realized suddenly that she had not yet closed the curtains. There was probably nobody out there, but probably was not good enough. She found her jeans at last under the dress. The curtains were *still* open. How many glasses of wine had she accepted? Thinking back, she realized that she had lost count. Her trainers were still beneath the chair. Stooping to tie the laces made her dizzy for a moment. She tried again with her head butting against the wall. She had done herself rather too well at dinner and she took an antacid tablet. She still felt slightly bilious but the chance to get rid of that inconvenient tree took precedence over any discomfort.

Dressed and shod at last, she donned the older of her two coats and picked up her rechargeable lantern. 'You may as well come along,' she told the spaniel. The words seemed determined to come out twisted, but she kept them firmly under control. Ellery seemed to understand her body language if not the actual words.

In the tool shed, she slung the heavy coil of nylon rope over her shoulder before setting off for the house again. She found that she had a tendency to walk round in a curve, but that must have been due to the weight of the rope. Once on the lawn, she made better progress although the lawn seemed to have developed some fresh undulations. She dropped the coil of rope at the base of the tree. The whole dinner party was emerging to see the fun. Cigar smoke hung in the still air, gleaming in the light shed by the lamps over the front door. There were glasses in evidence and Mr Henson was solemnly plying a decanter.

An argument had developed around the big four-by-four. 'I am not getting into the driving seat,' Will Largs said, firmly but politely.

'This isn't a public road,' Grant Wheatley pointed out.

'That has no effect in law. Members of the public have access. In fact, you are members of the public. If I were to back the car over one of you, I could be in serious trouble.'

'But it's all right if I do it, because I'm sober? Well, all right,' Jenny said. 'But you'll have to tell me what to do. Bob, guide me back.'

Will Largs joined May at the tree, where she was trying to hold the lantern while passing the end of the rope around the trunk. He took the lamp from her. 'Not so

33

high as to break it,' he said, 'but higher than that. We'll need leverage.'

'This is as high as I've got.'

The headlights of the vehicle came round, drowning the moonlight. Will put down the lamp, took her by the waist and, without great effort, lifted her up. Somehow his touch was friendly rather than intimate. It was a heady feeling like levitation and May, although she experienced a brief inclination to be sick over her supporter, was also tempted to prolong the moment and test his endurance by tying an endless series of half hitches. After a period lengthy enough to speak for his strength, he set her down gently. 'Are you sure that knot will hold?'

'You think you can do better?' May asked. 'I'll lift you up.'

Will gave a shout of laughter and paid out the coil of rope. It was long enough to reach clear of the grass. The big vehicle had been repositioned on the tarmac, facing the tree. He looked back to ensure that the tree could not reach so far before crouching to tie the rope to a towing ring. 'Select reverse,' he told Jenny. 'Four-wheel drive and lowest ratio. Then brakes off.' The vehicle crawled slowly backward. The rope tightened and then stretched. 'Now a touch of throttle.'

The rope came bar-taut. The tree swayed. May picked up the lamp and shone it on the trunk. There was no sign of a split. The tree groaned. The roots were beginning to lift, a gash like a grin circling the base of the tree. 'One good pull,' she called.

The engine note rose and there came a sudden yelp from the tyres. 'Gently,' Will said. 'Try rocking it.'

Jenny tapped a slow rhythm on the accelerator. The tree groaned more loudly and leaned a little further with each pull. The infant giant was fighting to hold on to its grip on earth. Then, with a swish and a tearing sound, it fell, a shadow across the sky, branches spreading softly on the grass and a ragged disc of roots rising from the earth. The air was filled with the smell of pine.

The roots on the lower side would still be anchored. 'Another yard or two,' May called. Obediently, the tree was hauled further across the grass, to the sound of crackling twigs and tearing root fibres.

May shone the lamp down into the hole, to assess the remaining roots. She expected to see a hollow of torn earth but some roots remained and they had assumed an extra-ordinary shape. They reminded her of some moviemaker's fantasy of the weird and horrible, seen on television and intended to send a shiver up the viewer's spine. Something out of a nightmare. A drunken nightmare. There seemed to be rotten cloth, falling apart. She blinked, but it did not go away. Through the gaps in the cloth and the matter beneath she could see white sticks. From a round shape which she had first taken to be a large stone pierced by two holes, teeth were grinning at her. She tried, unsuccessfully, to disbelieve her eyes.

'Hoy!' she shouted. 'Come here.'

'What's up?' replied a man's voice.

'There's a bod deddy.'

Ellery began barking.

The whole party began to converge on the upturned roots. Will Largs was the first to arrive. He took the lamp from May and shone it into the hole. The sight was no less horrid than before, perhaps a little worse now that she knew what to expect and had begun to believe that it was not some hallucination thrown up by a disturbed nervous system.

'Get back, all of you,' Will snapped. 'Bob, come here. And Jenny – you have a camera with you?'

'As always,' Jenny said. She seemed strangely calm.

The others retreated a few yards. It seemed to May that she had performed her part. The horrifying sight had completed the disturbance of her already upset stomach. She could feel a cold sweat prickling her face and her stomach was churning. She whistled a reluctant Ellery away from the hole. 'I'm going to bed,' she said carefully. 'I'll come up in the morning with the chainsaw and cut the trunk up into logs.'

'Just one minute,' Will said. 'You can't just find a body and go off to bed.'

May's head was swimming but she thought about it. Who was Will to order her about? 'Yes, I can,' she said at last.

Bob Welles looked into her face. Despite the poor combination of moonlight and lamps, he must have detected her unease. 'She won't run off, Sir,' he said. 'And this isn't yesterday's body. I doubt if there are many clues to disturb.'

Will hesitated. 'Oh, very well,' he said testily. 'Everybody else back in the house.' He produced a mobile phone. May had again called Ellery away from the hole and was making her way unsteadily across the lawn. Her sense of balance seemed to be deserting her. The bright blink of a camera flash pursued her. Faintly, she heard Will say something about some kind of a surgeon but she had lost interest. She was in a hurry to get indoors.

She had never been much of a drinker, but she recalled some advice and a very few experiences from her student days. She went into the bathroom and, without quite letting go of the basin, drank a large glass of water and sicked it up again. She then drank some more, washing down two aspirins.

In the bedroom, she began to undress but when she came to her trainers the laces seemed determined to tie themselves in knots. Her head began to swim and she had to straighten up. She tried to kick the shoes off but they were tight-fitting and ankle-high. As a last resort, she tried to remove her jeans over the trainers, but though the jeans turned inside out they were tight at the ankle and refused to come off. It was all too much. Her head was spinning in both directions at the same time, faster and faster. She flopped face down on the bed. In seconds, she was asleep.

She slept long and dreamlessly. When she became aware of bright light and a pulse in her head she pulled a pillow over her face and dozed again. She thought that she must have had a nightmare because the skeleton with half-rotted flesh and clothing falling away from the bones could surely not have been real. Such things just did not happen to ordinary respectable young lady gardeners. Although, when she came to think, rather woozily, about it, if anybody was going to dig up a body perhaps a gardener would be more likely to do so than anyone else.

She threw aside the duvet and got off the bed. She must have come to during the night, because her jeans were folded on the chair, her trainers were neatly disposed beneath and the duvet had been spread across her body. The curtains were still wide open and the overhead light was still on. The bedroom window looked on to a high wall backing the disused stables, where the polygonum that she had planted two years earlier seemed to be thriving. But when she forced herself to look obliquely to her left she could see, between the wall and the nearest greenhouse and through the greenhouse glass, a sector of lawn with white-overalled figures moving. Either it had been real or she was still dreaming! She drew the curtains almost closed, which, she admitted to herself, was locking the stable door. Her spectacles were on the dressing table. She peeped again between the curtains. The figures were undoubtedly policemen conducting a fingertip search.

She glanced in the mirror. No policeman, or anyone else, was going to see her as she was, or even with clothes on. She took a hot bath. She recalled that a prime cause of a hangover is lack of sugar. She had never felt less like eating but she breakfasted on a large bowl of well-sugared cereal and several cups of tea. She dressed as if for work and brushed out her hair by touch alone before she dared to look in the mirror again. Better, but not by a whole lot. Her hair seemed determined to stand up in fright. She tied it back in a ponytail. She usually wore make-up only on social occasions, but this was an emergency. She did what she could to repair the ravages of the previous evening.

Recognizing the signs, Ellery was waiting. When May opened the door, the spaniel shot across the yard and squatted before coming back to heel. May's stomach tried a tentative heave but settled again.

Walking steadily and being careful not to turn her head suddenly, May headed for the centre of activity. The light hurt her eyes until the sunshine darkened her Reactolite prescription glasses. Deep breaths of very fresh air went some way towards clearing her head. Somebody, she noticed, had coiled her rope neatly beside the fallen tree. The tarmac spreading before the front door now held neatly parked vehicles, some unmarked and some in two-tone livery. She recognized Jenny Welles, still in her party dress, standing among the men and handling some sort of camera. Ellery seemed drawn towards the hole but

May called the spaniel back to heel. Bob Welles came to meet her, still in his dinner suit without the bow tie.

'Who's in charge here?' she asked.

'I am, for the moment. The Super's gone back to Inverness.' His manner was still friendly but now it was more formal.

'Who?'

'Didn't you know? Detective Superintendent William Largs. And I'm Detective Inspector Robert Welles.'

'I never guessed. And Jenny? Is she a cop too?'

'No. But she's a photographer and often employed by the police when we're overstretched, as we usually are.'

He looked tired and unshaven. May detached her mind from her own woes. 'I don't suppose any of you had much sleep,' she said.

'Grant put a bedroom at our disposal, as well as a room for interviews. We managed an hour or two apiece between duties. We'll survive for a little longer. Your aunt and uncle were sent home long ago in the care of Mr Henson.'

'Can I cut up the tree and remove it?'

Bob half-closed his eyes and regarded the scene. 'I can't deny that it's in the way. We'll think about it later. First, let's take a statement from you.'

'If you're going to ask me about dates and things, I'd better fetch the diaries from the greenhouse.'

He looked at her in puzzlement. 'You keep your diary in the greenhouse?'

'The only things I really want to remember are exactly when plants were sown and potted and sprayed and pruned.' May left him and hurried to the nearer green-house. She collected a small stack of notebooks and school exercise books. Ellery had been following. May told the spaniel to stay and hurried back.

They walked towards the front door. There was one important topic which May felt should be cleared out of the way as soon as possible. 'Did you or Jenny visit my cottage during the night?'

'I was far too busy and Jenny was standing by to record anything that turned up. I think the Super went over that way to be sure that you were all right, while we were waiting for the SOCOs.'

May dragged her mind quickly away from the implications. 'I don't know what you must think of me,' she said quietly. 'I've become unused to drinking more than a half-pint shandy. The wine went to my head and other places. I hope I behaved.'

'Admirably, all things considered.' She could hear a smile in his voice. 'Compared to some I've had to deal with, you were a model of sobriety. I judge drinkers by two things – whether they drive a car and whether they get obstreperous. You passed on both counts. And anybody's stomach could well get topsy-turvy on being confronted suddenly by what you saw last night on top of a generous meal. We were rather a jolly party right up until you discovered the bod deddy.'

May was aghast. 'I didn't really say that. Did I?'

'We thought the expression rather felicitous. It seems to have found favour among the rank and file. You may end up in the *Oxford English Dictionary* yet.'

'I had hoped it was only a bad dream.'

They passed through the hall and into a modest room to the rear of the house. May remembered it as having been a snooker room, but one of Mrs Mellor's cousins had begged the table off her when she left Cannaluke Lodge. It now held three well-worn desks, presumably furnished by the Northern Constabulary. At one of these a uniformed female constable was working silently at a word processor, at another a man in plain clothes was sorting papers and making entries on some sort of chart. Bob – Detective Inspector Welles, as she must now try to think of him – showed May politely to a thinly upholstered stacking chair and seated himself in another across the third desk from her.

'You won't mind if we tape this? We'll pick out the salient parts later and give you a typed copy to sign.' He switched on the tape recorder that sat alone on the desk and told it the date. When he followed up with the time, May glanced incredulously at her wrist and realized that she had forgotten to put her watch on. Where had the time gone?

Bob Welles – she could think of him no other way – looked amused. 'Please state your full name and address,' he said.

After a moment's thought the required information came back to her. 'I am May Elizabeth Forsyth and I occupy the gardener's cottage at Cannaluke Lodge.'

'Where you are the gardener?'

'Yes.'

'When did you take up the post?'

May chose and opened one of the notebooks. 'Nearly three years ago,' she said. She chose her words carefully for the sake of the formal statement. 'I see that my first entry in the diary about working at Cannaluke Lodge was made on the fourteenth of August. That was on a temporary basis. The arrangement became firm about three weeks later. The previous gardener, Joe Scott, had absented himself and it seemed that he was not coming back. Anyway, Mr and Mrs Mellor made it clear that, even if he ever did return, they would prefer to have me, and I preferred gardening to any of the jobs I'd had before, so I moved into the cottage.'

'How long was that after he went away?'

May leafed back through the diary. 'About a month. I see that his last entry was made on the thirtieth of July.'

'He had been the previous occupant of the cottage? Had he cleared out all his personal possessions?'

May thought back. Her recall seemed to have been coated with treacle. 'By no means all. I noticed that there were no toiletries there – razor and toothbrush and so on – and his clothes were gone, but there were a lot of odds and ends left behind. And the place was dirty.'

'What happened to the odds and ends?'

'I put them into a carton. They're in one of the sheds. I don't have much storage space in the cottage. Then I scrubbed the place out and furnished it with odds and ends from home plus a few things that Mrs Mellor passed on to me.' She paused. The question could not be put off any longer. 'Was that his body?'

'For the moment, please confine yourself to answering my questions.' The Detective Inspector softened his words with the shadow of a smile. 'Did you know Mr Scott?'

'I'd met him, off and on. He'd been here for about five years and my home was not very far away. I was friendly with the Mellors. Joe was a good enough worker but not very enterprising about the design of the garden. They used to consult me. And I used to help Mr Scott occasionally. He wasn't jealous. Sometimes he even asked my advice.'

He looked at her with sudden interest. 'Advice?'

'Nothing personal. Just about the identification of unusual plants, soil chemistry, that sort of thing.'

'Tell me about him, as a person.'

'I'll tell you what I can. He is or was small for a man,

lean and muscular. Older than me but not by very much – perhaps thirty to thirty-five. His face was tanned from being out of doors so much—'

'Yours isn't.'

'I use face cream and a hat with a brim if there's a hot sun. He didn't. Bear with me, I'm trying to remember somebody who I never knew very well and haven't set eyes on for three years. If I use the past tense, it's not because of any guilty knowledge, it's mostly because I'm guessing that that's his body and, even if it isn't, he may look and be quite different by now. He had a soft voice and a country accent from somewhere south of here, Angus or Grampian perhaps. I don't think any of his features were memorable, but they fitted together to make one of those forceful faces. I'm sure somebody can produce a photograph of him, in fact I probably can if you want it, but it won't really reveal his eyes, which were his one good feature. They were clear and bright and, when they looked at you, you felt looked at. Does that make sense?'

Bob Welles turned his head. 'Does it?' he asked the woman PC.

She thought about it. 'Yes, Sir, I think it does,' she said at last.

'That may have been what women saw in him,' May said. 'He was certainly one for the girls, although he had a wife somewhere. I gathered that she had never taken to the area and they separated quite amicably. You never saw him out and about alone; there was always a woman in tow. How he met them I don't know, but those that he did meet he invariably made a pass at. He even came on to me once, but I made it clear that I'm aiming rather higher than a fellow gardener. I didn't admit that I had an intense dislike of him, because I was bound to meet him now and

43

again and there was no point asking for aggravation, but I thought that there was something nasty about him. There seemed to be others who weren't so fussy.'

Bob jotted down a note but seemed to decide that that subject had been covered. 'When you cleared out the cottage, did there seem to be any signs of female occupancy?'

'Not that I noticed, but I wasn't investigating him, just trying to get rid of his traces. Have a look in the box of oddments and you may spot something I missed.'

'What did the girls say about him, behind his back?'

May smiled wryly. 'I'm afraid I can't tell you, Inspector. They don't talk to me much. The village girls think I'm toffee-nosed and the ones I grew up with look down on me now because I'm only a gardener. Most of the gossip that I've heard, I've overheard; but none of it came from the mouths of women who'd been out with him, so I wouldn't suppose that he left any ill will behind him. And that's about all I can tell you, except that I think he must have had another source of income. We gardeners aren't noted for being dressy and around the garden he could be as scruffy as any of us, but when he was out with a girl he was definitely smart.'

'Now tell me about Janet Mellor.'

May allowed her surprise to show. 'Rather a mother's girl,' she said. 'Quite pretty, but you'll get plenty of photographs so you can judge for yourself. About my size and build but slightly fairer hair. She's one person whose attitude never changed when I came over to help with the work. She used to help in the garden, sometimes, along with her mother. She chatted with me from time to time.

'She seemed to regret a lack of romance in her life, but her mother was very protective and rather straight-laced.

44

You must know the sort, wanting to know who her daughter was going out with and what time she would be home. Latterly, however, Janet seemed more contented; and there was one occasion when she went off on her bicycle, saying that she was going to the shops with a girlfriend, but I was in a high part of the garden and I could see the road and she didn't go off in that direction at all. So young Janet may have been making excuses to sneak off and meet a boyfriend behind her mother's back and I can't say that I blamed her. Not long after that, she ran off. I drew my own conclusions.'

'Could you put a date to that?'

'Roughly.' May looked back through the notebooks. 'I remember that I was pruning my mother's roses when Mrs Mellor came down the garden to ask me if we'd seen Janet. That makes it the middle of March. Here we are. The eighteenth.'

DI Welles regarded May unseeingly while he considered. She waited patiently. 'That *sequoia* had already been planted when you arrived as gardener?'

'Yes. I'm sure that it wasn't there when I made my occasional visits, but when I took up the post, there it was. I didn't see it go in or I might have noticed how inappropriate it would be.' She flicked through the diary. 'I don't remember seeing any record of when it was planted.'

'Thank you. There will be more questions once we have a better idea as to what we want to know. For now, only one more. In your opinion, and disregarding any discrepancy of dates, is it possible that Miss Mellor and Mr Scott went away together?'

'In my opinion, absolutely and definitely no,' May said. 'He behaved flirtatiously towards her, but that was his manner towards every female. She didn't seem to have any more time for him than I had. I don't think that she was dissembling but, for all I know, that could have changed.' She paused and tried to verbalize a concept which was only just clarifying for her. 'A large part of female response, especially of younger girls, is to the fact of being wanted.'

This last revelation seemed to have given the Inspector food for thought. He reached out slowly and stopped the tape recorder. 'I'll have to ask you to stay away from your cottage for the rest of the day,' he said.

May gathered up her diaries. She was more interested in the implications than in being offended that her abode was to be searched. 'So you think that it's Joe Scott's body?'

'There has been no identification yet. Leave the diaries with us, please.'

He took the diaries out of her hand and escorted May back to the garden. The light hurt her eyes less than before. Outside the front door, they were alone. 'I can tell you this much,' he said. 'It will be all over the place by afternoon anyway. At first, we thought that it was the girl because it seemed rather small.'

'Joe Scott was small.'

'So we hear. Anyway, the body is definitely male.'

Detective Inspector Welles beckoned to the one man among the workers who was standing upright instead of down on hands and knees. The other man arrived with a brisk stride. He wore similar white overalls to the others but managed to be very neat, even to his neat moustache. 'Sir?' he said.

'This is Detective Sergeant Morrow. Sergeant, are we ready for the tree to be removed?'

'We've searched all round it. We want to see underneath but the SOCOs won't be too happy if the scene gets covered in sawdust.'

'I have a big nylon tarpaulin,' May said. 'The one we use to protect the grass sometimes, if we're digging. But it's no lightweight. And I don't know what you hope to find after three years of wind and rain.'

'We have to go through the motions. Any shortcuts can backfire later,' Bob Welles said with a fine disregard for his metaphors. 'I'll leave you with the Sergeant, then. Please give him the box of Mr Scott's bits and bobs.' He turned back into the house.

'It would amaze you what we do find, sometimes,' Sergeant Morrow said. 'Come with me, Miss, and point out what tools and things you want. Can't let you use your hatchet, I suppose. They'll want to test it for traces of blood.'

'Did—?' May broke off her question. She did not really want to know whether the Sergeant's reference to a hatchet stemmed from routine or from the nature of a wound in the skull. 'I don't have a hatchet,' she said. 'There wasn't one when I came here and I've always managed without.'

The lawn had been marked off into big squares with pegs and tape. Most of the men were on their knees, searching one of the squares. The Sergeant called out two names and two men joined them, seeming relieved to be on their feet. One was in uniform but the other, in plain clothes, was one whom May had seen occasionally in the district without ever supposing that he was a policeman. They walked together to the big tool shed. 'That rolled-up tarpaulin,' May said, 'those ear protectors, the goggles, the chainsaw, that round file and the can of two-stroke fuel. That's all right, isn't it? I take it that he wasn't chainsawn to death?'

'If he was,' said the Sergeant, 'nobody told me.' He looked at her doubtfully. It was quite common for murder

47

to be spoken of lightly among the police, as a defence against the constant acquaintance with death, but it was unusual among the general public. May was similarly defensive but, in addition, still only half believed the grisly snapshot glimpsed by the light of her lamp while her senses were fuddled. Her hangover, she thought numbly, was doing the talking. She reminded herself to keep a guard on her tongue.

May opened the adjoining, smaller shed and indicated a carton which had once held boxes of potato crisps. 'That's the box your Inspector mentioned. And can I use my Mini?' May pointed to her old Mini pickup.

'That's OK. It's already been examined.' The Sergeant saw May's eyebrows go up. 'We don't know where the body was brought from, Miss, nor how. It's routine to take a few swabs and scrapings from vehicles. And we do it quick. Once a crime's uncovered, the culprit sometimes panics and runs around clearing up any traces he might have left.'

Back in front of the house, the tree was lifted, with some difficulty, and the tarpaulin, after being examined carefully for possible contaminants, was dragged underneath. 'Leave the root-ball for the moment,' the Sergeant said. We'll have to sift every scrap of earth.'

May had rather dreaded what the noise of the chainsaw would do to her head, but the work proved almost painless and the familiar tasks made little demand on her surviving brain power. In twenty minutes, she had reduced the trunk and branches to their component parts. A few trips with the Mini removed the logs to the woodshed and the twigs and foliage to a bonfire site beyond the kitchen garden. The same two men helped her to dispose of the sawdust and return the tarpaulin and tools to the tool shed. She insisted on her small box of cleaning materials being brought out to her. Cleaning and oiling the chainsaw took only a minute.

'Can I get into my home now?' she asked Sergeant Morrow. 'Just for a few seconds?'

'Afraid not, Miss.'

May could sense a return of appetite. Something hot and greasy might help to settle her stomach. With new staff in the house and the police under her feet (and presumably wanting endless statements from the one person who had been in residence before as well as after the presumed events) Mrs Macdonald would have her hands full. 'Is it all right if I go down to the pub for some lunch?' she asked.

'I expect so. Better ask the Inspector.'

Bob Welles was standing over two men who were now scanning the area where the tree had lain. He greeted May with raised eyebrows and she asked her question.

'Yes, of course. You'll understand that we want time to examine the former home of the man who we're assuming to have been the body. Otherwise, we don't want to be more restrictive than we have to be.'

'And do you want me to keep my lips sealed about what I know?'

He produced a wry smile. 'Do you know anything we don't know?'

'If I do, I don't know it.' May's frown, which she felt had become established for the day, deepened. The conversation was getting out of hand.

'What you know, and what we know, amounts so far to a very small portion of damn-all. We may know more when we get the post-mortem report and a positive identification. Until then, we don't even know what we want to know. So tell them all you want. All I ask is that you bring

49

me back any potentially useful comments that you get in return.' He saw May's hackles begin to rise and made a small, pacific gesture. 'I'm not asking you to spy on your friends, although we wouldn't turn down any information that arrived by that route. But the little bits of gossip that would be helpful to us, like who was lusting after who and when, and who quarrelled with whom and so on and so forth. All those things will probably be common coin in the local chatter and very slow and difficult for us to gather up in the normal course of interviews.'

'I suppose I can do that much,' May said. They were still standing near where the tree had stood. The sky seemed empty. 'Now for a much more important question of my own. When can I replant this bed?'

He let a small chuckle escape him. 'You evidently have a clear idea of your priorities. I can't make any promises. We may have to keep what is obviously a crime scene intact for some time. All the earth will have to be sifted and after that it depends what, if anything, we've found.'

May sighed. 'During your sifting, I suppose you wouldn't care to incorporate some compost?'

'I'm afraid not.'

She sighed again. 'It sounds as if you're going to take half the summer. Ask your men whether any of them want to buy some pansies, just coming into flower and ready to plant out.'

Four

Before she could go to lunch, May had to knock on her own front door and, when it was opened by a detective or SOCO or possibly a forensic-science technician – she had no way of knowing which – beg him to fetch her purse, Ellery's lead and a handkerchief. Thus equipped, she fetched the spaniel from the greenhouse and set off on foot. She was not absolutely confident that she was ready to face the breathalyser yet, in fact she rather suspected that she would put the device off the clock.

A uniformed constable was on guard at the gate, a local man whom May had sometimes seen bustling importantly about the roads in a very small panda car. If May went that way, she would have to brave the media, who were so far represented by two patient reporters; but she had her own exit through an inconspicuous gap in the hedge at the corner of the garden. She had half a mile to walk along the grass verge.

Ellery walked resentfully on the lead. She would probably have stayed at heel but probably, in May's book, was not good enough and a rabbit might have tempted her across the road. The traffic was thin but tended to be going at speed. On any other day, May would have relished the fresh air, the birdsong, the view of the hills and the chance to stretch her legs; but now her stomach seemed to slap her backbone with every step and the view hurt her eyes.

The village had retained much of its identity. The pub, similarly, had suffered little change. Other inns might smarten and enlarge, offering lures to business lunchers, corporate entertainers and dirty weekenders, but the Firth-view Inn attracted only a small and unwanted share of that last market by virtue of its very modesty. Privacy and good value for money still had the power to attract. The proprietors, Luke and Mavis Ross, were modest, humble and content.

The facilities, which had evolved almost organically over the generations, included a small public bar for anyone deemed too mucky for more civilized amenities and an even smaller lounge which was rarely if ever used. There were two bedrooms. Life in the Firthview Inn centred mainly on the one big bar, catering to most comers. This was a cluttered room, the floor crammed with ill-matched small tables and bentwood chairs leaving only a space for stools along the bar and dangerously small space around the dartboard. The walls were hung with an extraordinary miscellany of curios, mainly antique agricultural and join-ery tools but including also items ranging from unusual bottles to what appeared to be a willow-pattern bedpan. A large fireplace usually filled the room with a not unpleasant smell of wood smoke while the heat drove drinkers away from that end of the room, but the fire had been allowed to go out for the summer, its place taken by a fan of iris leaves.

Outside the door, a painted sign advertised that hot snacks were served all day. A slightly more ambitious menu was available in the evenings, but at lunchtime the hot snacks were limited to those which could be provided by way of a toasted-sandwich maker, with whatever filling happened to be available at the time.

May gave the assembled customers a nod and a word of greeting to share between them. She took a hard wooden stool at the end of the counter. The combined smells of beer, food and tobacco smoke made her stomach squirm only slightly, which she took to be a good sign. She ordered two ham and tomato toasted sandwiches and her usual half-pint of shandy. Ellery went to occupy her favourite place under the dartboard, where, experience had taught her, she was never trodden on and any darts which hit the wire and rebounded usually bounced back clear of her. The rare puncture wound was accepted philosophically.

The Firthview Inn was an evening pub and the bar was often empty at lunchtime, but May guessed that the chance of some interesting local gossip had proved an attraction. Sporadic conversation among the seven or eight customers died as May entered and then resumed in an undertone. She waited to see who was going to open the batting.

The stool beside her was vacant but the next two were already occupied by a couple whom she knew slightly. Jim Ferrier had taken the only stool with a padded seat. He was well but casually dressed. He was both tall and stout with the beginnings of an overhanging belly. His handlebar moustache was in scale with the rest of him. He had worked for some years in the oil industry and was frequently employed as a consultant. The work took him to the Middle East and further afield, which explained his constantly tanned state, but between times he was often at home. May had always found him pompous, arrogant and patronizing, but without any real feeling of dislike because a sense of humour and a degree of intangible charm balanced his failings. Beyond him his wife, Margaret, looked small although she was taller than May and quite as heavily built. Her face was slightly flat but with a hooked nose, giving her the expression of a rather attractive owl.

Jim was usually loud in the backslapping manner. This time, however, he had clearly made up his mind to be circumspect. 'You've had some excitement up your way,' Jim said. May looked at him enquiringly. 'Oh, come on!' he said. 'We all saw the police cars going to and fro. Then there was an ambulance. And the milkman says that he was turned back at the gate. He had to deliver Mrs Macdonald's milk to a bobby at the gate plus an extra two bottles of gold top. What are the police saying?'

May was in a mood for being coaxed rather than pressured. 'Just questions,' she said. 'They asked me to be sure and tell them who was nervous enough to try to pump me.'

There was a momentary hush and then a small sound of amusement spread through the room. Jim looked put out and then acknowledged the joke with a half-smile. 'Oh come on!' he said again. 'This isn't nerves, it's pure, innocent nosiness. We know that there's a body. Do they know whose it is yet?'

'There's only two people gone missing from here,' Margaret Ferrier said. 'That's Janet Mellor and Joe Scott. Unless you count Daisy Hutchinson, who used to work in the pub here, but she travelled ten miles to work here every day. Her husband was sure she'd run off with that young aid worker who left to go to the Sudan.'

'It surely could not be Janet Mellor,' said a man in painter's overalls. He had a pronounced Highland lilt in his voice. May remembered seeing him at work on the

windows at Cannaluke Lodge. 'Everybody's friend, inof-
fensive as they come. And she never had to do with boys,
so it couldn't be that.'

May had been prepared to get the conversation going
but it had taken off of its own accord. She settled down to
listen.

'You're wrong there,' Margaret Ferrier said. 'It's not a
nice subject and I don't even like to talk about it, but a girl
doesn't have to be interested in sex before some man will
attack her. And then murder happens, almost as a matter
of course. Anyway, she did have a boyfriend, though she
kept very secretive about him.'

'I don't believe it!' the painter exclaimed. 'Such an
innocent-looking lass.'

'They're often the worst,' Margaret said.

'There was a rumour . . .' said May.

Mrs Ross was behind the bar. Despite spending a large
part of the day in the kitchen she was as thin as a rake, but
her hawk-like face belied a kindly nature. 'Well, it was true
for once,' she said. 'Don't you go repeating this, or if you
do don't say it came from me, but Mrs Mellor came in one
day for a bar lunch, as she did about once a week, and she
said that Janet had gone into Dornoch to the shops, with a
girl friend. I went into Bonar Bridge that afternoon and I
saw Janet in the street, alone. The direction she was going
didn't head towards the toilet or the bus.'

'That does not mean anything,' the painter said. 'The two
girls could have changed their minds and gone visiting.'

Mrs Ross shook her head. 'I know the signs. Furtive but
eager and walking happily, swinging her bum. She had a
boyfriend for sure.' Mrs Ross emitted a gusty sigh. 'If
that's her body up there, I like to think that she had some
joy in her life before she went.'

'You're a romantic,' Jim Ferrier said.

'I'm also a realist,' she retorted.

'I saw her in Bonar Bridge too,' Margaret Ferrier said. 'It stands to reason that a pretty girl like that isn't going to lack boyfriends, never mind a mother who thought she was still in rompers. Nature will have its way.' There was a murmur of agreement.

'Sometimes I wonder about you,' Jim said lightly.

His wife looked complacent. She could never have been beautiful and whatever looks she might have had were fading but she still had an air of femininity and a roving eye. May wondered whether she kept her husband guessing as a matter of principle. 'I saw Janet, too, in Bonar Bridge,' she said. 'She does seem to have had a fancy for the place.'

Charlie Mostyn, the farmer whose land adjoined the garden of Cannaluke Lodge, had a table to himself. He had finished his snack and was working on a pint of dark-looking beer. He had shed his customary dungarees and was comparatively presentable though his hands were stained. He was a man in his forties with an education behind him – she recalled hearing that he had given up college when he inherited the farm in his early twenties on the sudden death of his father by the explosion of a liquid-gas tank. He looked intellectual in a way, which was somehow out of keeping with his occupation, and this was emphasized by a pair of modern, frameless spectacles. 'And it couldn't be Daisy,' he said. 'From the top of my hill you can see the lawn at the Lodge and they were digging where that tree was that you wanted me to pull out, May. Daisy ran off years before that was planted. You couldn't plant a tree on top of a body without noticing.'

May shook her head. 'You could if you knew that it was there,' she said. She usually liked the farmer but he had the knack of irritating her from time to time by proving suddenly disobliging, just to show that he was still his own boss. She felt a touch of malicious mischief coming on. 'Charlie, why didn't you want to pull that tree out for me? You kept telling me to fell the tree although you knew that I wouldn't be able to plant a replacement for donkeys' years. And you said that your tractor was too busy, but I didn't see or hear it working today.'

'I was on the far slope.'

May pretended to look at him in disbelief. The farmer looked away.

'Couldn't be Daisy,' Mrs Ross said. 'I had Christmas cards from her, with foreign stamps on them.' She brought May her toasted sandwiches.

The man in painter's overalls evidently had a score to settle. 'You never did get on with Joe Scott,' he told the farmer. 'I heard the two of you going at it.'

Mostyn was looking black. 'Me and a hundred others,' he said. 'If I argued with Scott it was to tell him to stay away from my sisters. He was a bad bastard where girls were concerned and I kept him away from my two.'

'He took your Mabel to the pictures,' said a woman who seemed to be alone. She was a stranger to May but she evidently knew the farmer and took pleasure in joining in the needling.

'Just the once,' Mostyn said grimly. 'I damn soon put a stop to that. You don't seriously think I knocked him off and buried him, any of you? Doesn't make sense. Why would I bury him under the windows of the Lodge when I'd only have had to take the tractor and dig a deep hole on my own land?'

An elderly man, sitting alone in a corner, stirred. May seemed to recall that he was a retired lecturer. 'I'm not accusing you of anything, Charlie, but that argument doesn't stand up. If Scott was digging a hole for the tree and you fell out with him and killed him, it might well have been quicker and safer to pop him into the hole than move him on to your land.'

'Well, that's where you're wrong, Clever-clogs,' said the farmer hotly. 'That tree went in small, because I saw it, and small trees come in containers and they don't need much of a hole, nothing like big enough to bury a body in.' He drained his glass and left the bar, his every movement spelling resentment.

The elderly man got up and took the stool beside May. 'Would you take another?' he asked her.

May shook her head. She found shandy a wonderful refresher after a late night, but one was enough. 'Thank you,' she said, 'but no. This is my limit at lunchtime.'

'Well, I'm going to indulge myself.' He pushed his empty glass towards Mrs Ross. 'The same again, Mavis, please. They may not have made a positive identification yet, but can't you at least tell us whether the body was male or female?'

May had been content to listen and absorb, but it was time to stir the pot. 'I'm told that it was male,' she said.

'Joe Scott, then,' said Ferrier. He sounded pleased. Scott had not been popular.

'Not necessarily,' the elderly man said. May decided that he was the type to take pleasure in nit-picking.

Margaret Ferrier decided to support her husband – which, in May's experience, was not always the case. 'Joe Scott is the only man who's gone missing,' she pointed out.

'It could be somebody we don't know about,' said the

elderly man. 'Or, if you don't like coincidences, Joe Scott could have killed somebody and buried him and bolted.'

'And I wouldn't put it past him,' Mrs Ferrier said with feeling.

'Hullo!' Jim said. 'Did he make a pass at you?'

'All the damn time,' she said complacently.

'You should have told me.'

'You were hardly ever here. He never passed a woman without trying it on. You knew that, don't pretend to be surprised.'

A marital disagreement seemed imminent. Mrs Ross said quickly, 'I wonder who found the body.'

'I did,' May said. There was an immediate hush. May decided that she might as well extract as much social kudos as was available. 'We were having dinner at the Lodge. The policeman who's in charge of the case now was there as a guest with a simply huge four-by-four of at least five litres. I've been desperate to get that tree away before it got too big to pull, because it was going to grow several metres a year until it towered over the house, blotting out the light and sucking the moisture out of the ground.'

'Would that have mattered so much?' the elderly man asked.

'Well, yes, because it would have looked all wrong and it could have caused settlement cracks in the Lodge. So, with Charlie Mostyn letting me down, it seemed a good chance to get that tree pulled. The others stayed on the tarmac or were grouped around the car, but I stood by the tree. And as soon as it toppled, I saw it.' She shuddered involuntarily. 'And no, I'm not going to describe it to you. I'm only just beginning to believe that it was real and not a bad dream. Anyway, all that I really remember seeing was teeth.'

59

'Joe had good teeth. He was proud of them. You didn't see what he died of?' asked the lone woman.

'I didn't stand around looking.' May decided not to mention hatchets. She sought for a subject to turn the talk away from a topic which was begetting a return of her squeamishness, and found it. 'I can't think what induced Joe Scott to plant that tree there.'

'He can't have planted it on top of himself,' the elderly man pointed out.

May's thinking had not progressed that far. 'You're absolutely right. If it's him. He must have bought it,' May said. 'But I wonder where he meant to put it. I don't remember seeing it in the gardening diary.'

'I can tell you that,' Margaret Ferrier said triumphantly. 'I hired him to lop our trees – in his spare time, of course. When I said that I had to leave him to it because I wanted to go to the garden centre for a big bag of sphagnum moss peat he asked me to collect the tree, which he'd ordered by phone. It only came up to my waist at that time so it went into the back of the Shogun with room to spare. And that was just a day or two before he disappeared,' she added, 'because I remember saying to Jim that I was thankful I'd been paid for it before he went off.'

'I thought you were going to tell us where he meant to plant it,' said the elderly man.

Mrs Ferrier tapped her forehead. 'Going daft in my old age,' she said. 'Joe said that a tall tree would look well at the top of that hump above the water garden.'

'He could have been right,' May said, suddenly taken with the idea. 'Well, it's too late now, the tree was already too big to shift. I'll have to order another one if Mr Wheatley wants it. Funny, though. Joe wasn't usually that bright about the aesthetics of the garden. Things grew for him and he had a knack of planting them where they'd do well, but he'd not the least idea of making a natural-looking arrangement or a good blend of colours.'

'I think he said that it was Mrs Mellor's idea,' said Mrs Ferrier.

'If Joe Scott's body was buried,' said the elderly man, 'and a tree planted on top of it, there has to have been a reason and it can't have been robbery. Gardeners don't carry much money around.'

'He had more than you'd think,' Mrs Ross said. 'Enough to do a lot of drinking during the last few months. He often did come in here of an evening but not always to drink much, just to have a quiet word with people. Later, it was different. If you ask me, there was something on his mind.'

'He was up to something,' said the retired lecturer. 'I was always sure of it but I could never work out what it was.'

There was a feeling of amusement in the air, a consciousness of *I know something you don't know*, but May, looking quickly around, was not in time to see a smile on any particular face. The idea of Joe Scott being *up to something* did not require her to make any leap of faith but she could not imagine what it might have been. Gardeners, in her experience, lived circumscribed lives.

The company seemed to have run out of facts and speculation and to be looking expectantly at May, waiting for her to release a few more tantalizing fragments for them to chew, digest and excrete later for general gossip. But May suddenly felt a revulsion. Murder had no business intruding into the idyllic backwater into which she had settled. She wished them a good afternoon and made for the door.

* * *

From the roadway outside the Firthview Inn only glimpses of the Lodge could be seen through the trees, but from the hump of the bridge the widened part of the road giving access to the gates was almost in view. May could make out the tops of at least two vehicles and several human heads. A van bearing the insignia of a TV company was crawling along the road, apparently looking for the best viewpoint. The media, it seemed, were intrigued by the macabre nature of the mystery and were beginning to congregate. As the finder of the body she would be meat for them.

May had no intention of revealing her own secret access, so she turned the other way and beside the stone bridge over the burn she descended by a steep path to the farmland. From there it was an easy walk through two fields and along the banks of the Firth to enter the grounds of Cannaluke Lodge by way of the water garden.

She let Ellery off the lead. There were horses in the second field but the spaniel knew better than to approach them. The day was beautiful as only a day in spring can be although on the hills across the water the shadows of small clouds were in slow procession. There was little breeze but it was too early in the year for midges. May's hangover was melting away. There was blossom on the trees and, out on the water, a fish jumped.

They skirted the water garden, detouring around the hump where Joe Scott, according to Mrs Ferrier, had intended to plant the *sequoia*. Figures were still walking and crawling, but in a different area. May had a good view of her domain – the season of early bulbs was almost past but spring shrubs were in full flower, trees were coming into leaf and summer shrubs were beginning to explode into blossom. She really would have to separate the pink of the *ribes* from the red heat of the japonica, perhaps by something flowering white. A white lilac might do the trick. On the whole, the colours were almost as good as she could get them.

Despite her enjoyment of the results of her efforts, she was not at ease. She was unused to moving about the garden without at least a pair of secateurs and a small fork in her hand. Weeds would be germinating or spreading suckers. Young roots might be drying out. In the greenhouses, seedlings would become potbound or shoot beyond any possibility of transplanting. She told herself that she was thinking nonsense, that a day could not possibly make any difference. She could have taken Sunday off without compunction in accordance with local custom but, denied access to her tools, she thought that she could recognize the onset of withdrawal symptoms.

In her pocket, however, she had the polythene bag which she habitually carried against the rare event of Ellery sinning in the wrong place. Nearer the house she entered one of her favourite parts of the garden, where stone paving and drystone walls formed terraced beds and rock plants draped and tumbled down in a riot of spring colour. Here there was a bed of the small and very early *rhododendron praecox*. She sat Ellery and began work.

The spring sun was warm on her back. Gradually, the work performed its magic. She switched off, her mind drifting aimlessly among the early insects and the blossoms.

She was brought back to earth when a shadow fell beside her. She looked up. Bob Welles, now neat in a dark suit, looked enormous against the sky. 'What are you doing?' His enquiry sounded curious rather than suspicious.

'I am not burying another body,' May pointed out

tiredly. 'I couldn't, without access to any of my gardening tools. I'm deadheading.' Bob looked puzzled. 'Taking off the dead flowers *pour encourager les autres*. Is it all right if I empty my bag on to the compost heap or will you think that I'm covering up clues?'

'Don't be bitter,' he said. He smiled for a moment and became serious again. 'We can't let you have your tools back just yet. Will you come up to the house, please?'

'I suppose so,' May said in tones of great weariness although, in fact, she had almost finished the bed. 'May as well.' She got up and dusted her knees.

'We can go past your compost heaps.'

'Don't do me any favours.'

'I wasn't going to. We're going into a greenhouse anyway.' His voice remained cool and official.

No more than curious, May followed him. She emptied and pocketed her bag and sat Ellery outside the greenhouses. Bob led the way into the further greenhouse. The smell was of damp compost and foliage. He gestured around at the ranks of pots. 'These are all your plants?'

May was puzzled. 'To be precise,' she said, 'I suppose they're Mr Wheatley's.'

'You raised them from what? Seeds?'

'Seedlings are nearly all in the other greenhouse. These were raised from cuttings, mostly. And layers. They'll be planted out next winter; those that don't get sold or swapped for things we need from the garden centre. Why on earth are you interested in them? Nothing in here is more than two years old.'

Bob stooped and pointed under the long bench, where several spindly plants were managing to survive among the carefully hoarded pots and boxes and a collection of watering cans ready filled with water and coming to the temperature of the surrounding air prior to use. 'What about these?'

The question puzzled May but she attempted an answer. 'I can't have too many watering cans,' she said. 'So whenever there's a jumble sale or a car boot—'

Bob lifted his hand in a policemanlike gesture. 'Not the watering cans. The plants.'

'Weeds,' May said, 'in the sense that a weed is a plant growing where you don't want it. Again, why?'

'Do you know what they are?'

'No idea. Do you?'

'They're cannabis.'

'*What?*'

'Cannabis resin. Pot.'

'Well I'll be . . .' May refrained from expressing exactly what she would be. 'I never really looked at them, I just took it that somebody had tried to grow something like *Ricinus* and given up and they were still reseeding themselves and growing rank because of the limited light. They weren't in the way and the seeds never got up above the bench so I never bothered about them except to pull them up and throw them on the compost whenever I happened to think of it. I suppose the worms have been stoned out of their minds, if they have minds.'

Bob was not going to be diverted. 'What you're saying suggests that Joe Scott was growing cannabis plants in here.'

'Or somebody, but definitely not me. I'm not making any suggestions,' May said. 'That's your job. But I've just been told that he was in the habit of spending quiet evenings in the pub, talking to people but without drinking much until his last few months. That could mean that he was meeting customers.'

'True. Come into the house, please.'

Outside, Ellery rolled over for her. May stooped to give the spaniel the customary pat but her mind was absent. 'If I could use one of my forks,' she said, 'I could turn over the compost and see if we can still find any of the stems. That might give us a very approximate date. If Joe cleared out the cannabis because he meant to do a bunk, that's one thing. If it was earlier, it might mean that Mr Wheatley rumbled him and made him clear it all out.'

'Later, perhaps. Off the top of the head, I don't see that what we could learn would be relevant to our enquiries at the moment, but time will tell. As you said, drawing conclusions is our job. Come into the house.'

May followed again with her eyebrows up. They entered the house by a side door, leaving Ellery with strict instructions to stay. Bob Welles led the way into the former snooker room where he had interviewed her that morning. One of the large windows was up, admitting the spring air. The same two officers were still at work but they had been joined by Detective Superintendent Will Largs, who was leaning over the desk where the man in plain clothes was still attending to his charts. May was given a seat in the chair which she had occupied earlier.

'For purposes of elimination,' Bob said, 'we want samples of your fingerprints and DNA. They will be destroyed when this case is over.'

'Destroy them if you want to,' May said. 'Have them framed, for all I care. I've nothing to hide.'

The woman officer took May's fingerprints and helped her to clean the ink off her fingers. She let May take a swab from inside her own mouth before it was sealed in a glass vial.

Will Largs detached himself from the other desk and

carried another chair to join May and Bob. He greeted May in a manner nicely balanced between officialdom and friendship. Bob started the tape recorder and they went through the same rigmarole of recording the date and time and May's identity.

'Now,' Will said, 'I have to tell you that the body has been positively identified, by means of dental evidence, as that of Joseph Scott. You know what that means?'

May allowed a moment of silence to pass out of respect. 'Poor Joe,' she said at last. 'Not that I could think of anybody else who it could have been. I suppose it means I don't get back into my cottage just yet,' May said.

'I'm afraid that's true. It also means that we need a more exact timetable for the period before the tree was planted. But, first, some clothes had been buried with the body, along with a few personal possessions and toiletries, presumably to get rid of them and create the impression that he had left of his own accord. Can you tell us more about what you did and didn't find in the cottage when you took it over?'

May tried to think back to a period when she had been excited by the change in her lifestyle and looking forward to making a home of her own. She had been largely uninterested in the debris left by her predecessor. 'It was dirty and untidy. Joe managed to turn himself out smartly if he was going on the razzle but he was a bit of a slob at home. There was some furniture but it was worn and grotty. We moved it into the old stable – which is quite dry – and I suppose it's still there. I didn't notice any bloodstains on it, but you can look for yourselves. My mother gave me some furniture and Mrs Mellor was replacing some carpets and things and let me have them. I had to buy curtains.'

'Was the cottage locked?' Will Largs asked.

'Not when I came to look at it. I wouldn't know whether Mr Mellor had had to unlock it. As I told Bob – the Inspector, I should say – Joe's clothes and his personal effects had gone. I mean, I didn't find a razor or tooth-brush. I wasn't thinking about it particularly so I might have missed something that you would have found sig-nificant, but what I found seemed to be the sort of things a man might well abandon. Everything of possible usefulness I put into a cardboard carton, in case he came back, and you've got it. Obvious rubbish, and there was a lot of that, went out in the bin.' Will Largs looked pained. 'Well, I'm sorry,' May said. 'I didn't know that you were going to want it for clues, three years later. Anyway, I can't recall anything that you could have found in the least significant so there's no point asking me about it. It was just old newspapers and empty beer cans, that sort of thing.'

Bob Welles took up the questioning again. 'We found faint traces of blood on one spade and a fork. Can you offer any helpful explanation?'

May made a face. 'Only the unpleasant and obvious one,' she said. 'I mean, that they were used to bury him, or something like that. I don't remember anybody scratching themselves and bleeding over the tools.'

'Not to worry. That could have happened before your time. Traces can be detected after years have passed.' He hesitated but decided to move on. 'I'm afraid that we have difficulty making head or tail of these diaries.'

'I can't say that I'm surprised. Neither of us got top marks for legible handwriting and the diaries were only meant to be read by ourselves.' The diaries were on the desk in front of her and she selected one of them. 'These exercise books in the straggly handwriting were Joe Scott's.

68

He used sort of verbal shorthand but I had to learn to read it because I sometimes wanted to know when things had been planted and where he got them from. I see that the last entry was for the twenty-sixth of June that year and . . . Hold on a moment.'

She glanced back a few pages. 'While I was down at the Firthview Inn for lunch, Margaret Ferrier – she lives in the big house on the corner with all the ivy and the fancy hedge – she told me that she fetched the *sequoia* for Joe and that he intended to plant it on top of the hump above the water garden. Here it is, June the twenty-fourth. The *sequoia* doesn't seem to be mentioned again.

'I didn't make any fresh entries in the exercise books. The notebooks are mine. I have them going back for years, but when I came here I left my earlier ones at my mother's house and only brought the one which I had begun early that spring.'

Bob Welles was making notes. Will Largs glanced at the tape recorder to assure himself that it was running and that the needle moved with every sound. 'That's very helpful,' Will said. 'When did you last see Joe Scott?'

'Alive? About a week before he disappeared. Mrs Wheatley wanted my advice. Joe was going to put flowering broom into a particular bed and she didn't like the idea. I pointed out that he'd be forever weeding and he wouldn't be able use paraquat around there because the least touch of it is instant death to broom.'

'And when did you hear that he was missing?'

'Weeks later. Mrs Mellor phoned me to say that Joe hadn't been around for some time and there was some work that needed doing and would I come and lend a hand.' May referred to her notebooks again. 'That was on the fourteenth of August. About three weeks later, Mr

Mellor said that even if Joe ever showed his face again he wouldn't have him back, he'd rather have me. And I decided that I liked the life. Very little hassle and always something to show for my efforts. People are much harder work than plants, don't you think?'

Will nodded gravely. 'I can't quarrel with that. So the arrangement became a permanency?'

'Yes.'

May paused and waited, but Will Largs was frowning into space and Bob Welles seemed to be adding to his notes. 'Don't you want to hear what I gleaned in the pub at lunchtime?' she asked.

'Very much,' Will said.

May recounted the general discussion in the Firthview Inn in as much detail as she could remember. When she had finished, instead of the expected questions, Will Largs leaned forward and watched May's eyes. 'Miss Forsyth, can you account for your time between June the twenty-fourth and, say, the beginning of August?'

The idea that she might be thought to have any responsibility for the horrid thing below the *sequoia* tree was new and shocking to May. 'I *beg* your pardon?' she said coldly.

'We have to account for everyone who had any sort of connection with the dead man.'

May drew herself up but, for no reason that she could immediately explain to herself, without rising to her feet. Later she realized that standing up might have been reminiscent of standing before the head teacher's desk. Her hangover seemed to be flooding back. 'I assure you,' she said coldly, 'that I did not *connect* with Joe Scott in any sense except the purely professional. I never liked the man but I never wished him any harm. Why on earth would I want anything to do with killing him?'

Will Largs looked at her as dispassionately, she thought, as if she had been a fingerprint or a bloodstain. 'I never suggested for a moment that you did. But we have to eliminate everyone who might later be suggested. You must see that you inherited his house and his job and you could be seen to have your feet very comfortably under the table.'

Shock and belief were only now catching up with May. This was the last straw. She jumped to her feet and rested her knuckles on the desk, glaring at him. 'Superintendent, last night was the first time since I took up the post that I was ever invited to dine in the house, and that was because a guest was expected who, for very understandable reasons, could not find a date of his own. For your information, I went on a course on organic gardening at Stirling from—' she straightened up and consulted one of her notebooks '—from June twenty-third to the third of July. And I may say that I thought it was a load of crap. Good day to you.'

She made as dignified an exit as she could manage.

Five

May found herself in the hall. Several stuffed animal heads erected by some previous owner almost as long dead as the animals were staring at her, but they had become so familiar over the years that they no longer bothered her. She blinked back tears and scowled at the animal heads but they gazed back imperturbably. She had come to like the gruff policeman, almost to imagine a special empathy between them, but virtually to accuse her of doing away with Joe Scott in order to inherit his job and weasel her way into the favours of the household, that was too much. She gave herself a mental shake. No point letting people get to her. Work would be the cure.

She was wondering what useful work she could do without any of her tools and in the knowledge that whatever she attempted would only bring a policeman, nanny-like, to tell her to stop, when she heard a soft voice from on high. Twisting her neck and raising her eyes to where the elaborate oak stair met a landing that formed a gallery across one end of the hall, she saw Pauline Wheatley beckoning. Did she really want company? She decided that what she needed, for once, was an audience and that Polly was one of the few people with whom she felt able to speak freely.

'I'll come up in a minute,' she said. She slipped into the

downstairs cloakroom, ignoring signs that it had come into regular use by the police. With her cottage out of bounds for the moment she should, like royalty, miss no opportunity to relieve herself. When she had also blown her nose and washed her face and hands she emerged and climbed the stair. Polly was waiting at the door of what had once been a sewing room but was now furnished as a miniature parlour with several upright fireside chairs, one of which supported Grant Wheatley. A tea tray was set out on a low table. The room was decorated in neutral colours, suited to the selection of coloured threads, but it looked over the terraces and was altogether a more intimate and friendly room than the drawing room downstairs. It was also well away from the distracting presence of the police.

'When I heard your voice downstairs,' Polly said, 'I rang for Betty to ask Mrs Mac for another cup. It would have been less bother to fetch it myself but they both seem quite shocked if I lift a finger about the house. The Closed Shop principle, I suppose. Sit down and have a cup?'

'I'm in my gardening clothes.' May found that her voice was hoarse.

'You look clean to me. Anyway, I'm having these chairs re-covered.' Polly snapped her fingers. 'Clothes reminds me. I spoke to Mrs Mellor on the phone. I pointed out that the clothes in the trunk weren't the sort of thing the Bosnian peasants, or whoever, would find much use for. She didn't seem to want to talk or even think about it but she quite agreed that you should have them and a donation to Oxfam would do instead. If you're strapped for cash,' she added anxiously, 'I'll make the donation.'

May, once settled into a chair which, despite a bilious colour, she found more comfortable than the more opulent ones in the drawing room below, said that she would love a cup of tea. 'I can manage a modest donation,' she said, 'but thank you for the kind offer. You can top it up, if you like. I'm not proud.'

While his wife poured, Grant said, 'It's strangely inhibiting, having the police around the place, don't you think? Whatever happened was over long before we'd even heard of the place, and yet we can't help feeling that they're watching our every move, hoping to catch us smoking pot or something. That's why we're up here, out of the way.'

'To smoke pot?' May asked jokingly.

'That's not among our vices.'

'It's funny that you should say that about pot,' May remarked. 'What brought it to your mind?'

Grant looked at her in surprise. 'Nothing in particular. It was the only thing I could imagine the police suspecting us of.'

It took May all of a second to decide that that was reasonable. 'I seem to be getting as suspicious as they are,' she said. 'I just wouldn't advise you to say it again where they can overhear. It seems that Joe Scott or somebody raised some cannabis plants in one of the greenhouses. There are still a few seedlings coming up under the bench, only I was too innocent to recognize them – that's one species I'm definitely not familiar with. But there would have been time for me to raise a crop or two since I came here, so they probably think I've been setting up as a drug baroness.'

'No!' said Polly.

'Yes. That could explain why your friend Mr Largs suspects me of killing Joe Scott, or at least being concerned in his death.'

'No,' Polly said more mildly. 'You've got it wrong. He couldn't possibly think that.'

'He could, or something like it,' May said. She found that her tongue was running away with her although she was speaking through clenched teeth. She unclamped her jaw with a conscious effort and took several deep breaths. She was beginning to wonder whether she might not have overreacted. 'He actually asked me if I had an alibi for when Joe was killed.'

'In so many words?' Grant asked.

'Not exactly.' May thought back. 'He asked me if I could account for my time. And then he pointed out that I'd taken over Joe's job and his house. He was kind enough to mention that I seemed to have my feet under your table.'

'Well, that's not fair at all,' Polly said indignantly, 'when I had to twist your arm to get you to come to dinner at all. I'll tell him so, the first time I see him.'

May opened her mouth to beg her to do no such thing and then closed her mouth without speaking.

'They've identified the body, then?' Grant asked.

'So they tell me.' Bob Welles had more or less given her a *carte blanche*. May embarked on a résumé of what she had gleaned about the presumed murder.

She had nearly finished spelling out the few available facts when she was interrupted by a knock on the door. Bob Welles's head appeared. 'May I come in?'

'Please do,' Grant said, rising again. 'We've been waiting to be told when we can have our house and garden back.'

Bob settled in the one unoccupied chair. 'Not quite yet, I'm afraid. I really came for another word with Miss Forsyth.'

'Shall we leave you?' Grant asked.

'Not unless you want to. This is quite informal and I'd like to keep it that way. I have one or two questions for Miss Forsyth, but nothing confidential.'

75

'If you'll answer one or two questions for me,' May said, 'I may manage to be more helpful.'

The two men sat. Bob half-smiled. 'No promises, but fire away.'

'Can I get the use of my tools now?'

He hesitated. 'Some of them. We've removed certain items for forensic examination. What's still in the tool shed you can use.'

'Thank you. And what can I now get on with in the garden?'

'Nothing until the morning. Then ask me and I'll say yea or nay.'

'The lad should be coming to mow the grass tomorrow or the next day.' She saw doubt on Bob's face. 'I know you have your jobs to do, but the world doesn't come to an end—' She broke off. The choice of words was unfortunate because the world really had come to an end for Joe Scott. 'The lawns must have been mown nearly a hundred times since the . . . event,' she pointed out.

'True. That should be all right. I'll confirm in the morning.'

'And my cottage?'

Bob glanced at his watch. 'Give us a little longer.'

May turned to Grant Wheatley. 'This should be a busy time of year and I was getting behindhand before all this upset. May I take on the usual Work Experience young-sters? The headmaster always has a few who are never going to be academically inclined and he's only too happy for them to go out and learn something useful.'

'That will be all right,' Grant said. 'Give me a note of how many and how much. Polly and I may come out and lend a hand.'

May nodded loftily to Bob Welles.

'First things first,' Bob said. He produced an envelope. 'The Fatal Accident Inquiry will open, and be adjourned for sure, the day after tomorrow.'

Grant was frowning. 'That's a bit irregular, isn't it?' he asked.

'It's unusual in Scotland,' Bob admitted. 'But the Procurator Fiscal has more powers than most people realize and a great deal of discretion. This one has dual degrees – he worked for the CPS in the Borders for some years and he's fixated on the English system. The Sheriff was caught out once before when the then Fiscal waited for all the evidence to be in before calling for an FAI. There was another fatal accident involving the pathologist and a forensic scientist. Most of the testimony was on paper but much of the material evidence had been muddled up and it took them for ever to get other experts ready to testify. So he goes along with the Fiscal and gets the preliminary evidence on record from the start.

'This is your summons to attend.. As the person who found the body you'll be first on, but there's another inquiry before ours – an old man who died in his sleep. He hadn't been to a doctor in years, so there was nobody qualified to provide a certificate. I doubt if you'll be needed before eleven, but come at ten thirty, just in case. All right?'

'I suppose so,' May said.

Bob nodded, taking her words for confirmation. 'Next, from what you were telling us, you saw Joe Scott alive round about the seventeenth of June. Mrs Mellor was present. And Mr Mellor?'

'Yes.'

'What Mr Largs was going to ask you was whether all three seemed quite as usual. Or was there any tension? Anything said?'

May thought back. 'It's difficult to say. It was a long time ago and it wasn't always easy to tell with Joe. He was moody and he was the sort of man who was deferential to an employer's face and snide behind his or her back. I don't think that I saw him on his own that day. And Mr Mellor had had one heart attack a few months earlier, followed by the worry of their daughter running off, and he had his fatal heart attack later that summer. Mrs Mellor was worried sick about him. It was hardly the brightest time for them. They both seemed a bit subdued. I don't remember any atmosphere that wasn't explained by that. This was nearly three years ago, remember.'

Bob made a quick note but it was evident that his mind was elsewhere. 'Mr Largs didn't tell me to say this, but I could see that he was concerned when you took exception to what he asked you. It's always a problem when a case involves people who one knows socially.'

Feeling a little guilty, May found herself on the defensive. 'I didn't enjoy being suspected of something.' Even to herself, her voice sounded sulky.

'You weren't suspected of anything and, unless something really extraordinary turns up, you won't be.' Bob's manner had become quite fatherly, May thought, which she found quite unsuitable in somebody only a year or two older than herself. For two pins he would have patted her knee. 'Believe me, if he suspected you, Mr Largs wouldn't have tiptoed around the subject unless he thought that he could learn more that way. With anyone he seriously suspects he can turn into a tiger.' Bob grinned suddenly. 'He's never suspected his grandmother of anything worse than fiddling her Co-op dividend, but if he did, I'd expect him to tear her apart. But what you experienced was no more than routine. If we leave any gaps in our enquiries, defence counsel will certainly find them. They seem quite telepathic that way. He was only trying to fill in a gap in the chart.'

It dawned on May that Detective Superintendent Largs managed to inspire an unexpected affection in his men. She was feeling better. Her headache seemed to have disappeared altogether and even her stomach was quite settled. 'You can tell him that he's forgiven,' she said, almost under her breath.

'That's good.' Bob got up quickly. 'Thank you,' he said to nobody in particular.

'Poor man,' Polly said as the door closed behind him. 'He was quite embarrassed. And I didn't even offer him tea.'

'I doubt if he was short of tea,' May said quickly. 'They seem to be awash with it, downstairs. I think their panda cars run on it. They had extra milk delivered.'

'Don't try to change the subject,' Polly said. 'You've made a conquest. Just what Grant was afraid of.'

'Don't be silly!' This time, May's voice sounded unnecessarily vehement. She had recovered her liking for the big policeman.

'I mean it.'

'Polly's right,' Grant Wheatley said, twinkling. 'It must be the first time on record that a senior policeman sent a mediator to soothe a witness's ruffled sensibilities. I've seen Will Largs in action and he's the last person I'd expect to give a damn about a witness's feelings.'

'We don't know that he does give a damn,' May said. 'We've only got Bob Welles's word for it and it's probably all part of some fiendish police stratagem. Seduce the suspect into making damaging admissions. You read about it all the time.'

'Only in cheap thrillers,' Polly said, snorting with laughter. 'When you left the dinner table he said something to Jenny Welles about you being a more attractive young woman than the ones she'd been trying to set him up with. She told me later. I thought she'd been reading too much Barbara Cartland.'

'You were probably right.'

'We shall see,' said Polly. 'He's a very attractive man, even if he does look ogreish.'

That was going too far. 'He doesn't look at all ogreish,' May stated indignantly. 'Just sort of macho.'

Polly exchanged a wink with her husband. 'There you are, then. And now, let's go and arrange for that trunk to go down to your cottage.'

The searchers seemed to have finished with the grass. Two men were patiently picking earth off the upturned root-ball and sifting it. The others had moved to the beds. Their numbers were thinning. May cast up her eyes.

At least May could now see a task clear for the rest of the afternoon. She opened a new notebook. The first job for the Work Experience youths – and the Wheatleys, if they were as good as Grant's word – would be to fork over the beds, removing weeds but leaving the seedlings of the alpines and rock plants that she used as ground cover.

The tool shed was deserted. The police seemed to have made off with one fork and one spade. Presumably those would be the ones on which traces of blood had been detected. Fortunately, she had spares of a sort; and the garden centre would always lend her others in any emergency. She cleaned three plywood squares of the remnants from a similar exercise on the previous year. Each of these squares had been marked off in two halves, clearly labelled

80

as WEED and FLOWER. Then she went out with a tube of glue to gather samples of the leaves of any plant which could possibly cause confusion. On an earlier occasion a willing helper had carefully preserved examples of creeping buttercup and, worse, pulled out the seedlings of *saponaria* which May had been waiting to transplant. There would no longer be excuses for repeating such mistakes.

An overalled man was poking through the greenhouses. He seemed shocked at the idea that May might want to water her plants, but she went ahead anyway and dared him to try to stop her. After a brief absence, which she assumed to have been for a conference with Bob Welles, he left her alone and tried to ignore her coming and going while she refilled her watering cans.

There remained the problem of an evening meal. The Wheatleys, with consideration for their domestics but none for the outdoor staff, had gone out. Mrs Macdonald and the maids had already taken a high tea and had resumed the household tasks which had been impossible during the day. A visit to her cottage told her that white-overalled men were still trawling with sophisticated tools and chemicals for signs that Joe Scott had died, processed his cannabis or stepped over any of the other conventional borderlines there.

The two fixed points in May's universe were her flowers and the dog's dinner. At first, the man who answered her furious hammering at the door was uncooperative, but when she threatened to invoke not only the RSPCA but also her Westminster MP, her MSP and her MEP by name, he relented enough to bring out Ellery's bowl and a supply of dog food. (He was unaware that May had invented the names which she attached to those politicians. He had no more idea of their real names than she had.)

By now, her mother would certainly have been trying to reach her on the phone. She wondered whether she was strong enough to face up to an inquisition about the latest drama. Her mother would undoubtedly have heard a garbled version and have put her own interpretation on what she believed to be the facts. However, a duty visit was overdue and it would solve the problem of May's evening meal. She was probably below the breathalyser limit by now. She decided to give herself the benefit of the doubt. After all, it was only a few miles. She called from the phone in the Lodge hall.

With Ellery sitting at her side and peering interestedly through the windscreen, May steered her middle-aged Mini pickup out through the gates, greeting the guarding constable, a local man, with a queenly nod although he had twice pulled her up for ignoring stop signs. She turned left towards Bonar Bridge. The media had seen their fill, given up in disgust or gone in search of victuals. For once she had no need to pander to her mother's prejudices, but she had borrowed a brush from the hall of the Lodge and attacked her jeans until they were relatively soil-free. Her striped shirt she wore loose for partial concealment of what she had not been able to dislodge.

She did not have far to drive. After a few miles, she turned right on to a road which wound steeply uphill between trees and occasional fields, with intermittent houses. Her mother occupied a comparatively modern bungalow (originally built for a now defunct market garden) which her father had purchased for his retirement. May's occasional suggestions that her mother would be more convenient to the shops and other facilities in Dornoch or Bonar Bridge were never well received. As long as she could drive a car safely, her mother said, she would remain in the house she knew and look out over the view she loved, at which times Ellie Mathieson, the carer and companion, would exude disappointment.

May parked in the short driveway, facing the doors of the single-car garage where lurked her mother's totally unsuitable Land Rover, originally the purchase of the doctor who often needed its off-road facility. May had several times offered her mother a swap but one look at the Mini was more than enough, and the Land Rover did have the advantage that other drivers steered well clear of Mrs Forsyth's eccentric driving.

May left Ellery in the Mini with the windows slightly open. The garden looked shaggier than she remembered, but she was prepared neither to criticize nor to do anything about it except to put one of the Work Experience youths, at her own expense, to clearing the weeds on the rare occasions when the two ladies went away. This service was never acknowledged and probably not even noticed. Ellie answered the door, a late-middle-aged widow becoming pleasantly plump, with lank hair somewhere between fair and grey.

Mrs Forsyth was in the kitchen, fussing over the finishing touches to the meal that Ellie had prepared. This proved to be a light meal but no more so than May was accustomed to taking. May was able to forestall criticism, by complaining that she had not been allowed into her cottage to change her dress. They sat down almost immediately. There was wine on the table in honour of May's visit but May, whose palate was becoming tuned to the crumbs falling from the Wheatleys' table, put it down as chateau Co-op and, remembering Jenny Welles's example, limited herself to a small glass on the excuse that she was driving. The fact that she could easily have left her car and walked back to Cannaluke Lodge passed unremarked.

Mrs Forsyth was showing early signs of Parkinson's disease and she ate with care, but her mind was still alert with only occasional intervals of vagueness. Her manner, however, was inclined to be plaintive. She waited until they had begun the meal before opening with, 'I've been trying to phone you all day, ever since we heard the news on the morning radio. Your phone seems to be out of order.'

'Probably off the hook. I've been kept out of my cottage,' May reminded her, 'and I don't suppose that the police felt like acting as my answering service.'

At the mention of the police, both ladies flinched. Mrs Forsyth added a sigh. 'I always knew,' she said, 'that no good would come of you working as a common gardener.'

'After all the money you spent on my education,' May added for her. It had been a recurrent theme. 'Mother, I am happy there. Don't you want me to be happy?'

Mrs Forsyth froze with a forkful of food shaking in the air. 'Don't be silly, dear. How can you be happy, digging up dead bodies?'

'It's only happened the once,' May pointed out. 'I don't make a habit of it. You probably haven't heard yet, but the body has been confirmed as being Joe Scott.'

The news produced a flutter of interest but Mrs Forsyth was not diverted for more than a few seconds. 'I don't like you getting mixed up with the police.'

'I am hardly "mixed up" with the police.' May paused but decided not to admit that there was one policeman with whom she could happily be *mixed up*. 'I only went to work at Cannaluke Lodge because Joe didn't seem to be around any more. But I've been occupying his cottage and working where he worked, so of course the police have to search in those places and ask me some questions. They're interrupting my work but otherwise it's been quite interesting.'

Ellie put down her fork. 'On the lunchtime news,' she said in her rather prissy Edinburgh accent, 'they showed a photograph of the superintendent in charge. Have you met him? He looks a holy terror.'

'Actually, he's rather nice,' May said. 'He's a keen gardener. He was asking me how he should prune his rambler roses.'

This domestic slant seemed to reassure Mrs Forsyth and she diverted, as often before, down memory lane. 'I remember the day when Violet Mellor came to tell us that Mr Scott had disappeared – "run off", she said – and to ask you to help her out. It was only going to be temporary.'

May recognized a danger signal. The question of her career was about to raise its head again. 'She thought that he'd run off? Why did she think that? Did she say anything else?'

Mrs Forsyth was proud of her memory and always seized any chance to show it off. 'She said that she wasn't in the least surprised, he'd always been a flighty type, and he'd been moving around from job to job all his life. And she wasn't too disappointed – he was a good enough gardener in a public park sort of way but he had no imagination and there was something sly about him. You were out, you remember, and Violet and I had quite a chat while we waited for you to come home. But she was really much more concerned about Janet and her husband's deteriorating heart. He was having quite frequent attacks of angina and he wouldn't carry his spray or his pills. Violet was very worried.'

'Rightly, as it turned out. What did she think had happened to Janet?' May asked.

'She was quite sure that Janet had run off to have a baby. As a matter of fact,' Mrs Forsyth said, lowering her voice, 'we still meet for a coffee now and again and she still clings to that hope. She said that Janet had talked a lot about that. Janet didn't seem particularly interested in having a husband or even in motherhood,' Mrs Forsyth said disapprovingly. 'It was the act of maternity that seemed to fascinate her. Vi had noticed certain signs – no appetite in the mornings and that sort of thing – and she was sure that Janet had deliberately got herself pregnant, but before she could bring herself to talk about it Janet had vanished suddenly and Vi convinced herself that the girl had run off to have the baby. Her great concern was that she might have had the baby adopted before Vi could get hold of her and tell her that she'd love to have a grandchild on whichever side of the blanket it was born. I think Vi also had a particular husband in mind for Janet but that went by the board and he's married somebody else now. Anyway, he would have been totally unsuitable.'

Here there was a digression for several minutes as Mrs Forsyth identified the young man and counted the many reasons why he would have been unsuitable. (May had to agree. He would have been a disaster. He had been jailed for causing a serious accident while drunk, and as soon as he was no longer around to cover his tracks it had emerged that he had been embezzling from his employer.) 'Of course,' she resumed, 'as the months went by she lost hope that Janet would walk back in. Either she had died in childbirth or she was living with the man and was never coming home. I suggested that she advertise – "All is forgiven", that sort of thing – but I don't think that she ever took my advice.'

This was all very interesting, but the demise of Joe Scott was of more immediate concern. 'Had anybody ever enquired after Joe Scott?'

Mrs Forsyth's head nodded regularly as a matter of course, but now she gave a nod which was too definite to be a symptom of her Parkinson's disease. 'Vi said that his wife came asking, when she stopped hearing from him. I suppose that means when the money dried up. Awful woman! An accent you could have chopped logs with and I don't think that country life agreed with her. She ran off back to Torry or somewhere soon after Mr Scott took the job here. I remember Mrs Scott as being fat but Vi said that she had become quite gross.'

May had had her meal and had gleaned such crumbs of information as were going, but she was not allowed to escape before the two older ladies, while uttering exclamations of horror and disapproval, had extracted every detail about the finding of the corpse and May's subsequent experiences of the investigation. Mrs Forsyth was loudly regretful that a prior undertaking to host the local Craft Club would prevent her from attending the Fatal Accident Inquiry in order to watch her daughter clearing the legal hurdles which she was sure would be put in her path. Mrs Forsyth was still a devoted reader of Perry Mason.

May glanced surreptitiously at her watch. The police must surely be finished with her cottage by now. Or, if not, it would surely be reasonable to expect them to make other arrangements for her. She excused herself as soon as she dared and drove home. Her cottage was dark and locked up. She had to walk up to the Lodge for the duplicate key.

Six

Bob Welles, May had learned, was for the moment occupying a room at the Firthview Inn. Next morning, however, he had gone into Inverness to fetch a change of clothes and to confer with Will Largs – who, May was told by a chatty Detective Sergeant, was technically the Senior Investigating Officer but had several other though lesser cases to worry about.

In the absence of either of the senior detectives, May found herself unable to get any sensible comment from the officers left in charge as to where she could and could not get back to work. She waited until two men had completed their scrutiny of a rocky slope above the water garden and then spent a useful day there, weeding and then planting out in the shade of a large beech the *vinca major* plants saved from under the *sequoia* tree. The police might be a nuisance and be treading down her beds and marking the grass, but at least they seemed still to be fending off the media.

Mrs Macdonald was now assisted by two regular maids in training, supplemented by a cleaning lady from the village. The housekeeper complained bitterly that the two girls absorbed more of her time in instruction than they saved her with their work, but it was noticeable that she was run less far off her feet than previously. Thus she had time to provide lunch for May as well as the maids.

May fended off all demands for a detailed description of the body but told the others what little she knew about the progress being made by the police. Mrs Macdonald confided that she had already confirmed to the police May's assessment of the relationships between the Mellors and their gardener at around the time when Joe Scott had disappeared, but she became tight-lipped and disapproving when the question of any possible romance on Janet Mellor's part came up. She had accepted the Wheatleys but she still had a fierce loyalty to the Mellors. What Janet might or might not have done was not a subject for kitchen gossip. Joe Scott was a different matter altogether, but she had held herself aloof from mere gardeners until the arrival of May who, as the daughter of the late doctor, had an uncertain but definitely higher status.

That evening, May delved into the trunkful of Janet Mellor's clothes and selected a cotton dress in blue and white as being suitably flattering but not too frivolous for a Fatal Accident Enquiry. There was even a pair of thin tights but, when it came to shoes, Janet's feet had been smaller and May's own shoes would have to do. Fortunately, however, she spent most of her days in Wellingtons or trainers, depending on the weather, so that her old shoes, although not up to current fashion, were little worn. While passing an iron over the dress, she considered sending off her donation to Oxfam straight away but decided that a delay would be only sensible. Janet might still turn up some day, demanding the return of her clothes. Gardeners are not well paid and, although her cost of living might well have been envied by one of the peasants assisted by Oxfam, May was still being pursued for repayment of the tail end of her student loan and the Mini pickup was unlikely to pass any more

MOTs. Her own need of the money was not so very far short of Oxfam's.

Next morning, the day of the Fatal Accident Enquiry, she was interrupted before she could begin by the arrival of Duke Ellon to cut the grass. Bob Welles had left word that mowing the lawns would be in order. Duke was a fair-haired and gangling youth, still subject to teenage acne but nevertheless already showing looks which would soon make him irresistible to the girls with whom he was showing signs of preoccupation. She read him her usual lecture about preparing the mowings properly for compost, knowing that he would, as usual, forget; but his shortcomings were now balanced by an apparent lack of interest in dead bodies.

There was still a police presence in the makeshift incident room. She was in the process of leaving a message with the sergeant in charge, to the effect that young Duke had been about the garden during what were presumed to be Joe Scott's last days on earth and might prove to be a source of information, when word reached her that two Work Experience youths, one male and one female, had arrived by bus from the secondary school.

These she introduced to her information boards. She spent some time explaining that she wanted the beds which had been defiled by the police searchers forked over carefully, the plants and their seedlings left untouched, the weeds removed and *not* buried but collected in the green bags and *not* added to the compost. She added that she would rather have one small bed done properly than all the beds given a short-term cosmetic rake-over. The girl seemed to be taking in the message and she thought that something useful might be achieved if they could keep their hands off each other. From the look of the boy, this was unlikely.

Back in the cottage, she changed, scrubbing her hands, dressing and making up with care and adding a modest pair of earrings that had been a gift from her mother. She would, after all, be in the public eye.

Dornoch, where the FAI was to be held, was a twenty-minute drive away. The interior of her Mini pickup was usually lightly dusted with loam, compost, dry dung or a variety of agricultural chemicals, transferred inside, a little at a time, on her hands, feet or clothes. She had planned to give it its biennial valeting before trusting the dress to it, but the Wheatleys felt a proprietorial concern in the mystery and Grant had offered her a lift in the Jaguar. May left Ellery in Mrs Macdonald's care, warning the latter sternly not to overfeed the bitch. Ellery, knowing Mrs Macdonald for a soft touch, observed her mistress's departure complacently. May and Polly travelled in style, sitting together in the back of the sumptuous car with Grant at the wheel.

Conversation, in the back seat, roamed over the weather, gardening and clothes. May confessed to being nervous about her forthcoming ordeal. 'I'm out of practice at speaking in front of a lot of people,' she said. 'Gardening's a solitary sort of life.'

Grant spoke over his shoulder. 'You've been a lecturer. And Mrs Macdonald says that you take visitors on conducted tours of the garden in summer and do it very well. I hope you'll go on doing that. I'd feel very selfish and dog-in-the-manger, keeping the pleasure of it all to ourselves.'

'That never adds up to more than half a dozen at a time,' May said. 'And then I'm speaking on my own subject to people who want to listen.'

'You'll find this much the same,' Grant said. 'They want to hear what you have to say and you only have to talk

91

about what you know. In fact, you mustn't suggest anything you don't know to be true. Just answer questions, as
asked, clearly and simply and, if you don't know the
answer, say so. You'll do fine.'

'Grant knows what he's talking about,' Polly said comfortably.

They passed Skibo Castle and joined for a mile or two
the wooded road north towards John o'Groats, only to
turn off almost immediately on to the road through
Camore to Dornoch. Under the sun the stones of the
old town showed warm tones of brown and grey.

May was much better acquainted with the geography of
Dornoch than either of the others. The parking spaces
outside and opposite the Sheriff Court were unusually full.
She directed Grant round two corners to park behind the
cathedral and they walked across the grass and under the
trees. The Sheriff Court was the middle of three old
buildings, flanked by the sixteenth-century Dornoch Castle, now a hotel. The Victorian court building had a
vaguely ecclesiastical look.

'You should get a chauffeur,' Polly told her husband.
'There wasn't much point making money all these years if
you don't let somebody else do the worrying and the
parking and then still have to count your drinks.'

'I like driving,' Grant said. 'I don't get to do much for
myself these days.'

'You could always make the chauffeur sit in the passenger seat on the outward trip,' Polly pointed out.

'You're finding early retirement a bore?' May asked.

'A little.'

'Don't you believe him,' Polly said. 'He's just got an idea
for a new virtual-reality game which will keep him out of
mischief for years. He says it'll knock their socks off. I

thought he was going to retire and take it easy, but I'm not sure that he could have been happy in idleness. He's a workaholic. Like yourself.' May was startled to realize that the description of her was a fair one.

They entered the building under the eye of a TV camera. The glass eye followed them – library shots, she presumed, for later use if any or all of them should turn out to be responsible for the corpse. May was diverted into a waiting room. This already held several people and more were trickling in. She was surprised to discover that there was not a single familiar face until, from scraps of overheard conversation, she realized that one of the strangers had been called to testify at the Fatal Accident Inquiry still in progress and others at the trial to follow of three youths who had indulged themselves a little too well and had driven a stolen combine harvester through the town and along the main road, abandoning it in the grounds of Dunrobin Castle.

She sank into a reverie. She was wondering whether she should pollinate the fruit trees by hand that year, or if she could safely trust the insects to undertake that essential service, when her name was called. She was led to a witness box in a courtroom resembling a large, Victorian class-room, into which had been crammed uncomfortable-looking pews for several officials and the public. Only the Sheriff had been treated with more consideration. Several of the audience had notebooks on their knees and she assumed them to be reporters.

May took an oath and confirmed her name, address and occupation. Glancing around, she saw the Wheatleys near the back of the room and Margaret Ferrier watching her raptly from a position near the reporters.

The Procurator Fiscal took up the questioning. He was a

small and bristling man who seemed to be restraining an excess of nervous energy. 'The garden of Cannaluke Lodge appears in the background of several of the police photographs. It seems to be exceptionally beautiful. Is that all your own work?'

As the Fiscal intended, May immediately felt at ease. 'I sketched the original layout, so the garden had shape when I took up the post although I've made many alterations to the planting. I've spent my time moving things around to fill in gaps and make better seasonal arrangements of colour.'

That, it seemed, was enough chat. The Fiscal got down to business. 'Please tell us how the discovery of the body came to occur.'

May embarked on an explanation. She refused to allow occasional questions to upset her as she explained the reasons why she had wanted the tree to be pulled rather than felled.

'That tree was *in situ* when you took up your post?'

'It was small and seemed to have been newly planted at that time. Then, quite recently, I was glancing over my record photographs of the garden and I noticed that the tree had shown remarkable growth. I looked at it more closely and realized that the species was *sequoia*, the giant redwood, which grows quickly to about three hundred feet in America, rather less in Britain. Its position, not far from the house and the dining-room window, would soon have become totally unsuitable. The farmer was unwilling to bring his tractor, which he said was too busy.' May had considered getting in a dig at Charlie Mostyn but decided to let it go for the moment. 'On the night in question, I was invited to dinner at the Lodge.'

'Is that not rather unusual,' enquired the Sheriff, looking

down from his elevated position, 'inviting the gardener to dinner?'

May decided that he was only filling in the record and not patronizing her. 'Very. But perhaps I'm a rather unusual gardener,' she suggested. There was a ripple of laughter. 'Anyway, my employers had guests coming and there was a spare man, so they insisted that I attend to make up the number and I allowed myself to be persuaded. I was partnered with a gentleman, a Mr Largs, who I now know to be a Detective Superintendent though I was unaware of it at the time.' A ripple of interest and amusement stirred the room. 'He had arrived in a powerful four-wheel-drive vehicle and I suggested that it could pull the tree for me. He helped me with the rope and somebody else drove the vehicle. The tree was pulled over without great difficulty, upending the roots and leaving a hole.'

'And you were the first to see the body?'

'That's so. You understand that this was by the light of the moon, one lamp and the vehicle's headlights and even the headlights couldn't shine down into the hole. I thought at first that I was seeing a chance pattern of roots and stones, but then I recognized bones and teeth and I called out. Mr Largs came immediately and was joined by another guest, also a policeman.'

'What happened next?'

May had no intention of admitting that she had been too tipsy to stay around. Adhering strictly to the truth, she said, 'I don't know. I was upset. It had been a shock. I went and lay on my bed until the morning.'

'Very understandable, I'm sure,' said the Fiscal. He picked up a paper and studied it. 'I understand that you had dug around the roots of the tree to loosen it, in readiness for it being pulled down. In the process, you gained no inkling that there might be a body there?'

'None at all.'

'You didn't feel any resistance? Or – forgive me – smell a smell?'

May refused to think back. The idea repelled her. 'If I felt anything,' she said, 'I put it down to a root. I did not notice . . . the other thing.'

The Procurator Fiscal nodded. 'I think that's all. Very well. You may step down, Miss Forsyth, but please don't go away. There may be further questions.'

Nobody seemed to expect her to leave the room. Having said her piece she was presumably free to hear the other witnesses. She looked around for a seat and caught Grant Wheatley's eye. He signalled with a small movement of his head and she saw that the Wheatleys had kept a space for her. They squeezed together to let her in. The pews were as uncomfortable as she had supposed.

The next witness was a dentist, a well-upholstered lady unknown to May, who confirmed the corpse's identity from a comparison of its teeth with her dental charts.

Detective Superintendent Largs was being called. Will Largs, very neat in a good, grey suit, entered through a different door and took the stand. May had not set eyes on him since she had flared up, unreasonably as she could now see, and bitten his head off. But his eyes found her and she thought that he half-smiled. She no longer saw his craggy looks as in any way unattractive but was beginning to recognize or imagine an underlying benevolence.

Will's version of the finding of the body agreed with May's. He testified that he had immediately called for the police surgeon, the pathologist and others and had remained in personal charge of the investigation. He passed lightly over the more gruesome details but explained that the remains of clothing and personal possessions, including a razor and toothbrush, had been found around and under the body.

'Does that suggest that he had been about to leave the area? Or that somebody wished to give the impression that he had done so?'

'In my opinion, the latter.'

'Did you see any wound on the body?'

'Not at that time. I left the body undisturbed pending the arrival of the pathologist.'

The Sheriff looked up at the large wall clock. 'This would seem to be a suitable time to adjourn for lunch. You may stand down, Mr Largs. We will resume at two.'

Grant and Polly Wheatley carried May off for lunch, ignoring her half-hearted protests. In the hall they passed Will Largs. There was no smile this time but the pursed lips of displeasure which, added to his formidable features, left no room for doubt about his feelings. May decided sadly that, though she might have forgiven him, he had not after all forgiven her.

They went in to the Castle Hotel next door. The dining room was far from empty but Grant, with just the right mixture of friendliness and command, obtained first a table and then prompt service.

'I wonder why the Sheriff told me to stick around,' May said nervously. 'I don't know what else I can tell them.'

'There's probably a lot, if they knew it,' Polly said. 'All the local gossip and history.'

Grant shook his head and swallowed his mouthful of scampi. 'Gossip and history are for the police to gather up and present to this or another court. The job of the Sheriff is to decide whether somebody's dead, and who, and whether it was murder or accident or suicide. Sometimes they add a rider about culpability or balance of mind. In England, very occasionally, they point the finger at a killer, but they're not supposed to and it's not usual. I don't suppose you'll be needed.'

'Thank God for that!' May said. 'I was expecting the Sheriff to smite me with a thunderbolt if I contradicted myself.'

Grant nodded sympathetically. 'I'm given to understand that this particular Sheriff thinks himself quite capable of striking witnesses with thunderbolts, but don't worry about it. He's deluding himself. They don't usually hold Fatal Accident Inquiries until they're ready with the verdict so this isn't the usual course of events, but I don't see that they can do anything but adjourn for the police and the Fiscal to complete their enquiries. We'll find out this afternoon.'

'They won't do what you said, will they?' May said. 'Name the murderer, I mean. I hope to God not. It's only just beginning to dawn on me that he was almost certainly murdered, and by somebody I know.'

'But not necessarily,' said Polly. 'I mean, not necessarily murdered.'

'He didn't bury himself under a tree,' said her husband.

Polly frowned at him and then glanced mischievously at May. 'There are other possibilities. Think about this. Somebody killed him accidentally – backed a car over him or something. Rather than face the music, they buried him and planted the tree on top.'

'Ingenious,' Grant said. 'Unlikely but ingenious. Who do you have in mind for the culprit?'

Polly was almost hugging herself with enjoyment.

'Somebody local. A driver. Somebody who knew where to get the tree and the tools and who could dig in the garden without anybody thinking it odd.'

May realized that her leg was being pulled. The sensation had become unfamiliar during her years of solo working but it was pleasantly reminiscent of her student days so she refused to be provoked. 'And why would I then have the tree pulled out again?'

'Three years later? You said yourself that the tree was in the wrong place and you would have been sure by then that there was nothing to connect you with the remains.'

May laughed. 'As Grant said, very ingenious. And if you say any part of it within earshot of the police, I'll write rude words all over your lawn with weedkiller.'

'They're my lawns too but I wouldn't blame you,' Grant said. 'Come to me if you want any help with the rude words.'

Will Largs was not called back to the stand as soon as the hearing resumed. Instead, the first witness of the afternoon was a round and balding man whose name May immediately forgot. He identified himself as the pathologist. He stated that he had examined the body in place and then removed it to the mortuary. There, he had at once constructed a dental chart of the deceased, which the police had taken for purposes of identification. He had then proceeded with his autopsy.

The body was that of a man in his early forties. Death had occurred between one and six years earlier. It was impossible to be more precise after so much time. The ground was unusually dry, probably due in large part to the demand for moisture made by the growing tree. (He went into some detail about the processes of putrefaction, adipocere and mummification and the activity of insects, which few of those present understood and May, in particular, tried not to hear.)

The body, he continued, had suffered several wounds but he had concluded that the fatal blow had been struck, to the victim's head, with a sharp instrument such as a hatchet or tomahawk. Other damage had been inflicted, long after death, to the front of the skull and body, possibly by means of a spade. In answer to a question from the Sheriff, he agreed that the damage had been consistent with somebody digging above the body, unaware of its presence. (May felt the eyes of the room upon her.)

The pathologist concluded his evidence by commenting on the deceased's general state of health, which seemed to have been good, and the absence of detectable traces of toxins in the body. He was excused.

May was suddenly called again. Her heart, or some other organ, seemed to have jumped into her throat but she swallowed it down while she walked forward. Her footsteps seemed to echo around the courtroom. In answer to the Fiscal's question, she said, 'When I took over the tools, there was no hatchet to be seen. I thought of obtaining one but I was generally well equipped in all other respects and never had any great need of it.'

'Was there anything to suggest that there had ever been a hatchet among the tools?'

May was about to protest ignorance when a memory returned to her. 'I remember seeing Mr Scott use a hatchet once, a long time ago, but whether it belonged at Cannaluke Lodge, or was borrowed, or was his own property and he sold it, I have no idea. Most of the tools had their own places and there was an empty clip on the wall that might have been for a hatchet. It might equally have been for some other small tool that had been lost or borrowed and not returned.'

She was thanked and told that she could go, but she resumed her seat with the Wheatleys.

Detective Superintendent Largs was then recalled. He advised the Sheriff that enquiries were continuing and that many items discovered in a search of the area were being examined to see what further clues might be obtained. He asked for an adjournment to allow the police to continue their investigation. This was granted and the next case was called.

May, Polly and Grant slipped out. The cameras seemed to have gone.

While Grant went to fetch the Jaguar, Polly and May were intercepted by Will Largs. May was ready to cringe but the big man, far from being aggressive, was almost apologetic. After thanking Polly again for the dinner, he turned to May. 'I thought that this might be a convenient time to invite you for that look at my garden,' he said with clumsy formality.

'I would have liked that, but I don't have my car with me,' May said. 'And the buses are impossible.'

'But of course I'd bring you back home.' Will looked surprised that she should suppose anything else. 'It's only about an hour's run. Would that be all right?' he asked Polly.

'Yes of course,' Polly said smugly.

'I'll bring my car round.' He made off across the road almost at a trot.

'There you are,' Polly said. 'What did I tell you? I bet he invites you to dinner.'

May was aware of her own heartbeat but she spoke lightly. 'I bet he doesn't. It's either "Will you walk into my parlour" or "Once aboard the lugger", and I don't know which I fear more. Nobody's given me a chance to say whether I want to go.'

'That's because we all know the answer. What have you got to lose?'

May shrugged helplessly. 'Nothing I haven't lost before, I suppose. Will you take a look at those youngsters for me? Make sure that they're actually working instead of carrying on among the shrubs?' At that moment Will's enormous car loomed round the corner. 'And explain to Grant for me,' May added.

'Yes, yes and yes. Now go,' Polly said. 'Have fun. But not too much fun. And I'll see you tomorrow.' Her smile became a broad grin. 'Unless of course . . .'

'Put it out of your indelicate mind,' May said.

The big four-by-four pulled up beside them. Will Largs came out to open the door for her. As the car moved off with an easy surge of power, May said, 'I hope this isn't a cunning plan to get a suspect into your toils.'

Will managed a laugh. 'Nothing like that,' he said. 'This is purely social. I've been working long hours for days and I feel entitled to a little leisure time. My cases can run themselves for an afternoon.' He drove in silence until they were back on the main road and heading south. 'Having said that, I'll ask one question. Who could tell me if there ever was a hatchet in the clip you referred to?'

When she came to think about it, May was almost sure that Joe Scott had been hired to replace a predecessor who had died suddenly of a stroke. Joe and Mr Mellor had gone to join him. 'I can only suggest that you try some of the Work Experience helpers from before my time. Duke Ellon, who still comes to cut the grass, might remember.'

'Thank you.' Several miles went by in silence. 'I mustn't say too much about the case,' he resumed suddenly, 'and I'm not going to apologize for doing my job. If I was clumsy, put it down to the fact that I wanted to clear the air and be free to meet you again socially.'

Any faint residue of May's resentment melted away. 'Well, I'm sorry I flared up. It caught me flat-footed.' She grabbed at a change of subject. 'Did I do all right in the witness box?'

'Admirably. You could have been doing it all your life. I hope that I passed muster.'

'You're joking?'

'Not at all.'

'I thought that policemen were so used to giving evidence that they took it in their stride.'

'Not me. When you've had as many maulings from defending QCs as I've had, you can get a bit punch-drunk. There were no lawyers there to represent possibly interested parties, but sometimes at a Fiscal's inquiry – or an English inquest – you get barristers, even senior QCs, representing clients who think that they might be implicated later in something nefarious. They want to pick holes in every fragment of the police evidence, just in case.'

'Well, I thought that you came over loud and clear,' May said. 'I'd have believed you even if I hadn't known that you were speaking the truth.'

They crossed the long bridge over the Dornoch Firth. Golden gorse gave way to the strident yellow of oilseed rape. May was not accustomed to being a passenger but she soon relaxed. Will was a good driver. The A9 north of Inverness does not lend itself to overtaking and is often encumbered by slow vehicles, but he had the confidence and reflexes and his car had the power and brakes to take advantage of any gap in the oncoming traffic. He kept up a rapid pace. May guessed that his car was well known to his colleagues in Traffic and ignored by them, while Will seemed to know the location of any possible speed trap or working camera. After the slow grumble of the Mini, it could have been a new world.

They reached and ran alongside the Cromarty Firth but at the roundabout before the bridge Will took the road for Dingwall. He sensed her surprise. 'I live in Beauly,' he said. 'It's not many miles from Inverness and only a hundredth of the traffic.' The road became cosier, fringed with trees. They were running through pastoral land but after Muir of Ord May could glimpse jagged hills and distant mountains.

The small town of Beauly spreads picturesquely beside its own river. Will's house turned out to be an upper-quality, medium-sized bungalow on the edge of the town, overlooking a single field and the river beyond. His garden was surprisingly large and at first glance May decided that it was lovingly tended by an owner who was limited in both knowledge and time. They walked round slowly and May, first making sure that advice really would be welcomed rather than resented, limited herself to hints about labour-saving techniques of planting and maintenance. Suggestions for improving the unimaginative layout, she felt, would be construed as criticism.

There was a teak seat on a terrace above the small lawn and they sat to enjoy the sunshine. 'What were you saying,' Will asked, 'about organic gardening being a lot of crap?'

May had regretted words spoken in the heat of the moment and which had been intended to shock. 'Partly, it was just a silly pun,' she admitted. 'Organic gardening has its place. But so has the use of chemicals in the right place and the right season and in the right doses. You don't want to use an insecticide where you want pollination, or paraquat near broom or anything else it's going to kill dead, or certain fungicides near any of the hydrangeas, or moss-killers in calm, hot weather. On the other hand, some ass assured the course that if you leave your roses alone the ladybirds will come and eat the greenfly. I tried it and they didn't. I'll give you a photocopy of a chart that spells it all out.'

'I'd appreciate that.' He glanced at his watch and May noticed that the afternoon seemed to have gone past in a rush. 'I'd make dinner for us, but I keep a bachelor house. We can do better than convenience meals.'

'I don't mind TV dinners,' May said.

'You must depend on them all the time, as I do, but I'm not going to foist another one of them on you. I promised you a good meal and when I invite a lady to dine, which doesn't happen very often, I make it an excuse to eat properly. Let's go into the house for a minute.'

He led her in through a French window. The sitting room was very clean and tidy, almost surgically sterile. There were few ornaments and no photographs at all. Will gave her a sherry and excused himself. She could hear his voice from somewhere nearby.

Looking around, May noticed that an easy chair facing the large television showed signs of use but that the furniture was otherwise pristine. A bookcase stood handy to what was obviously the favourite chair. No detective stories, of course, and no romances, just humour and adventure. With sudden insight, she visualized the life of a widower, going reluctantly home to an empty house and frozen meals. A life rather like her own, in fact. All reminders of his late wife were out of sight. He had seemed to be on close terms with Bob and Jenny Largs. Did they, she wondered, invite him to their home for meals? Was there any warmth in his life?

Will came back. 'We have a table,' he said. He helped himself to a glass of tonic water, seated himself in the more worn armchair and glanced around as though seeing the room for the first time. 'I have a cleaning lady who comes in twice a week,' he said. 'If I leave anything out she tidies it away and I may not see it again for months. That's the only reason that the place is so tidy.'

'That's a good reason,' she replied. 'But without it, what would the room be like?'

He considered the question seriously. 'Not terribly different. I wouldn't call myself tidy, but I'm methodical. I like to know exactly where everything is. I leave things in place until I've finished with them and then I put them away. And you?'

'I'm the other way round. I like a place to look tidy but I know that whatever I throw away today I'll be in dire need of next week, so I tend to have cartons of old treasure in whatever attic space I may have.'

He nodded approvingly. 'Those are excellent characteristics in a witness. Or, of course, in a criminal or in somebody whose death may have to be investigated. Which reminds me. There was one other question I meant to ask you. I think I've usually seen you wearing glasses.'

'That isn't a question and I'd love to know whether you're considering me a witness, a suspect or a possible murderee, but yes. My eyes aren't too bad. I have one long-sighted eye and one slightly short-sighted and only slight astigmatism, so I can manage without my glasses, as now, but I can't tolerate contact lenses, I dazzle easily and my glasses are Reactolite so I wear them most of the time.'

'You always wear those horn-rims?'

'They're all I've got. I'd like to afford some more modern frames, but I comfort myself with the thought that they give me a misleading look of intelligence. Why do you ask?'

He smiled, the warm smile which had attracted her on the night of the dinner. 'I don't think there's any doubt about your intelligence. Now if I don't answer your question you'll read all sorts of implications into mine. A left-hand spectacle lens turned up in the earth under the tree. It could have been there for many years, of course. There was nothing high-tech about it. The lens was smaller than yours but the prescription was only a little stronger.'

'You checked my prescription?'

'We're checking everybody's prescription whose name figures in the case, so don't get on your high horse again. Unfortunately, half the world seems to be slightly myopic with no astigmatism to speak of. You, however, are the other way round. I was just making sure that you hadn't dropped it. Mr Scott never wore glasses?'

'I never saw him wearing them.'

'Nor did anyone else that we've spoken to so far. Our table should be ready in a minute. Shall we move?'

He locked the French window and escorted her out of the front door. The front garden was small and formal with a beautiful weeping ash central to a small plot of grass. 'It's only a step,' he said. 'Shall we walk?'

May was not wearing the shoes that she would have chosen for walking but she agreed. He took her arm very gently – quite unlike the grip that he would have applied in an arrest, she told herself. The restaurant was around the corner but only a hundred paces away. The proprietor greeted her host by name and showed all the signs of

107

pleasure and surprise at her presence. Either it was a male conspiracy or, if Will Largs dined there, it was usually alone.

He turned out to be a far better host than she had expected. He consulted her about her choice of wine and then ordered a whole bottle from the upper end of the price bracket. Were senior officers breathalyser-proof or was he going to send her home by panda car? Or did he not intend her to reach home that evening? What she had seen of him in the process of his work suggested that he was well able to express himself. On the evening of the Wheatleys' dinner he had seemed rather tongue-tied but now, as his reserve wore off, he chatted freely and amusingly about the affairs of the day and the life of a police officer. The wine was excellent, far better than would usually fall within a gardener's budget but May had no intention of being seen as a lush. She contented herself with two glasses. The bottle seemed to empty itself all the same. That again suggested that he did not intend to drive her home. She felt a tremor in her knees.

'Did your late wife enjoy your garden?' May was bold enough to ask.

Will's smile became grim. He lowered his voice. 'My ex-wife is still very much alive, more's the pity. Between ourselves, if she turned up under a root-ball I should not complain. She had a great power to attract but she made my life a misery for years. By the grace of God there were no children, so when I discovered that she was playing fast and loose with some of my colleagues it was more a relief than otherwise. I divorced her without the least compunction. We were incompatible. I was an atheist and she was the antichrist.'

May considered the implications of the comment. 'You can't get less compatible than that,' she said at last.

He chuckled. 'I knew that you were intelligent and had a sense of humour. I like that about you.'

'Is that all?' she asked before she could stop herself.

He glanced around to be sure that the staff and the other diners were not within earshot. 'By no means,' he said. He reached for her hand and she was too slow to pull it away. He looked into her eyes with an intensity that made her feel hollow. 'I like you as a person and I find you attractive. Your features are good. Real beauty is so often spoiled by remoteness, but there's something in your expression, even in repose, which is more captivating. The promise of friendship, I think. You don't mind my talking like this?'

May managed to shake her head.

'It must be the wine talking. Well, let it talk, because I want you to know. Without being skinny, your figure is delectable – I can think of no other word. And you shouldn't wear trousers.'

'They make my bum look big?' she asked anxiously. The wine had loosened both their tongues but she began to fear what might pop out.

He shook his head impatiently. 'If anybody ever says that of you, I'll set them straight. No. But they hide your legs. You have pretty legs. I am becoming devoted to your legs.'

It seemed that any inhibitions had floated away on the wine. Perhaps it was time for a little restraint. 'They are rather fond of each other,' she said huskily.

He looked at her thoughtfully. Had she gone too far? Or had he missed the implication? But he laughed, suddenly and joyously. 'Beautifully said! You mean that they don't like to be parted. Never? Or not on such short acquaintance?'

'The latter.' She felt that she was still straying into deep water. To her relief, the bill arrived. 'Perhaps you would see me safely on to the bus,' she said tactfully.

He laughed again. 'You'll get the lift that I promised you, but I've no intention of taking the wheel again today.' He looked out into the darkness. 'Jenny Welles should be along in a minute. Strictly between ourselves, she thinks, quite wrongly, that I was responsible for Bob's promotion.' He put money, quite a lot of money, down and the waiter whisked it away. 'After my divorce, my position was untenable. I had the chance of a transfer up here with promotion and I jumped at it. My predecessor had taken early retirement and there was something of a cloud hanging over his more likely successors. I had been sent up here to investigate some allegations and seemed to have got on well with the powers that be. I brought Bob with me but his promotion was on merit. We've had to learn a lot of Scots law and procedures, but I think it's been a good move for both of us. Bob and Jenny live not far from here.'

The big four-by-four drew up outside a few minutes later. Jenny remained seated at the wheel. They went out. Will was about to put May into the front passenger seat, but Jenny said, 'You two get into the back.' When they were comfortably seated and the car was in motion she added, 'Now you can canoodle away all you want.'

That effectively killed the conversation for most of the way back but Will captured May's hand. May was conscious that, after years of gardening, even conscientious use of hand creams had not saved her skin from becoming rough. She could have pulled her hand away but it would have been unkind to let him suffer any feeling of rejection. All kinds of messages were passing by way of that contact. Will had managed the outward journey in barely over an hour but the return trip took much longer. Jenny was a good but less inspired driver.

May decided that she was in no hurry. As they crossed the long bridge over the Dornoch Firth, she said. 'I'll have to return your hospitality. Would you like to come over for dinner on Sunday evening? I'll have that chart ready for you by then.'

He gave her hand an extra squeeze. Really, they were behaving like a couple of teenagers but it seemed somehow appropriate to the moment. 'I'd like that,' he said. 'I'll bring some wine. You're sure that it's not too much . . . ?'

'Trouble? Certainly not. Expense? Don't worry about it. We'll have pheasant. I always have pheasant on Sundays.'

'Really? You must—' He stopped abruptly.

'Must be very well paid for a gardener?' May suggested. 'Not really, though I don't complain. I'll let you into the secrets of my economy. In the winter, when I'm less busy, I go beating or picking up for a local shoot and get given a brace of pheasants each time. I buy more pheasants in the feather during January when they're well grown and the price is rock bottom, skin them myself and put them away in the freezer. One pheasant does me for Sunday and Monday and sometimes Tuesday as well if it's a big bird. Most years I pay fifty pence a brace and the keeper's quite happy because that's as much as he gets from the game dealer.'

'But that's a ridiculous price,' Jenny said.

'It is. But the British housewife has never caught on to the fact that pheasant is good poultry with no additives and no salmonella. So the supermarkets treat it as a luxury item. Come again later in the year and I'll give you trout. I spend almost nothing on meat. Or fruit or vegetables. I have a good air rifle and any rabbits or pigeon that think they can raid the garden end up in the freezer. What I don't eat, plus scraps from the house, go towards feeding Ellery. That's Highland thrift for you. Jenny, would you and Bob like to come on Sunday?'

'I think so,' Jenny said. 'I'll ask Bob. If you don't hear from me tomorrow, you're on. And thanks.'

'Come in the afternoon and I'll give you the conducted tour of what's left of the garden after your cops have done their considerable worst to it. I usually expect a tip, but on this occasion I'll let you off.'

'I don't see why,' Jenny said. 'You've just given me a valuable tip. Come January, can you put me in touch with a keeper near Beauly?'

'I can ask around,' said May.

The big car pulled up in front of the Lodge. Will got out and walked May to her door. They were out of sight from the car. It was immediately clear that neither knew what the other hoped or expected. After a few silent seconds, May thanked him for his hospitality. He took her hand and she thought that he was going to kiss it. She wondered whether to kiss his cheek. They shook hands and he turned and hurried away.

Seven

Most of the police had departed at last, leaving only a token presence in the temporary incident room where Bob Welles remained in command. Kitchen gossip suggested that he was receiving and collating reports from a number of officers still engaged on house-to-house enquiries.

To May's surprise, the boy and girl had done a job which was, if not faultless, at least well above average. The police had left the bed where the body had been found in a state of turmoil with a central crater. When the youngsters arrived for a second day she congratulated them and, prior to moving them on to the kitchen garden, set them to reinstating the bed. Any damage to the grass would have to wait. The root-ball had been cleaned of earth and stones and was easily reduced to a tidy stump which was man-handled into May's pickup and dumped at the bonfire site.

It was May's chance to get compost mixed into the earth. Between the greenhouses and the kitchen garden wall was a double row of enclosures, back to back, built of timber slats. One row held compost, the other leaf mould. May fetched a barrow. Her favourite spade was still in the hands of the police, but there was a shovel in the shed and she began to fill the barrow with well-rotted compost.

It was another bright morning. Perhaps they were going

to get a good summer for once. Her mind was miles away and the barrow was almost full of the rich, chocolate-brown compost when the shovel clanked against another metal object. She gave the shovel a twist and a rusted blade surfaced. For a moment, the significance escaped her. It would have been easy enough for some gardener to lay down a tool and, after it was covered by fresh deposits of compostible material, forget just where. Even a cook depositing scraps might by mistake have included some utensil. She was on the point of picking it up when her mind awoke with a start.

There was a plastic tag nailed to the back of the container. Scrawled on it in felt-tip was a number. She glanced at its legend. She left the shovel and the blade where they were and backed away as if from some evil presence. She felt the fine hairs crawling up her back and yet she had no intention of having her activities frozen again by the police. She trundled the barrow to where the youngsters were working. The hole had been filled and they were preparing to dig over the bed. She gave them their instructions. Then she sat Ellery and went into the house.

Bob Welles looked up from a stack of papers – reports or statements, she had no way of knowing – and he smiled at her. 'Jenny said to tell you that we'll come over on Sunday with the greatest pleasure. And thank you. Four-ish?'

'Earlier if you like, unless you're already sick of the sight of the garden.' Though big with news, May felt that it might be difficult to get Bob's full attention once she had unburdened herself. 'There's something I was going to copy for Will Largs. I was going to ask Grant Wheatley to do it for me but I see that you have a photocopier here.'

'No problem. Bring it in.'

114

Her own business disposed of for the moment, May returned to the purpose of her visit. 'You'd better come with me,' she said. 'I've found something that may interest you. First let me look in the diaries. They're back here?'

He took the diaries out of a cabinet and she found what she wanted within a few seconds. Without asking superfluous questions, Bob followed her out through the side door and blinked in the sudden sunlight. At May's whistle, Ellery pranced to join them.

The rusty blade, as May had guessed, turned out to be attached to a handle, the whole forming a domestic but formidable-looking hatchet. Bob retained his professional aplomb but she could see the excitement reflected in his body posture. 'Did you touch it?'

May refrained from asking him whether he really thought that he was going to find fingerprints on it and contented herself with saying, 'No. But I must have moved it with the shovel.'

'What can you tell me about it?'

May arranged her thoughts. 'As far as I know, I never saw it before, though I remember seeing Joe Scott using a hatchet rather like this one a month or two before he disappeared. From the diary, I see that he started this compost heap in the middle of the April of that year. And I opened a new heap the following September. That thing could have been there since Joe was . . . killed. I would have turned the compost over several times, but the hatchet was near the bottom so I suppose I could easily have missed it. Somebody wanting to hide it in a hurry would have pushed it well down into the fresh compost.'

'The compost at that time being what? Weeds?'

'I don't put weeds into the compost, nor did Joe. Some do, but I think it's too easy to make a rod for your own back by including seeds or roots. You can't count on the latent heat of decomposition to kill them all. You have to take your chances with grass seeds in the lawn mowings. I'd expect the compost to include kitchen refuse, cut grass, prunings and torn-up newspapers. And leaf mould from a year or two earlier.'

Bob, who was evidently not a gardener, was looking slightly stunned by this excess of information. 'I see,' he said at last. 'You'd better leave this lot alone. The forensics lads will have to see it in situ, for all the good that will do, and sift through the rest of the heap.'

Sifting would not do the compost any harm. The police had their job to do but May had hers. 'Tell them to chuck out any twiggy material they come across. I'll get on with drawing my compost from the next heap,' she said. 'It wasn't started until three or four months after Joe disappeared, so there's no more likely to be any clues there than buried anywhere else in the garden. I'll tell you if I come across anything. When do I get my spade and fork back?'

If Bob was about to make an instinctive protest against any more compost being removed, he was distracted by the question. 'Not for some time, I'm afraid,' he said. 'Faint traces – very faint traces – of human blood were found on each of them, in the joint between wood and metal. If the spade was used to bury Mr Scott, blood could easily have got on to it that time. You can't offer any explanation for blood on the fork? Nobody gashed themselves and bled over your tools?'

'Nothing more than a scratch from a thorn, to my knowledge. Possibly, in Joe's time. You'd better have a look back in the diaries or have me look for you – I'd expect any such incident to be recorded. Traces of blood can be detected many years later, can't they?'

116

'I'm afraid so.'

'Will they be able to get useful DNA out of those traces after such a lapse of time? I'm sorry,' May added quickly. 'I've no business asking you that sort of question.'

Bob shrugged. 'I couldn't answer that anyway. I think the scientists are working on ever more sensitive techniques.'

A gardener's work is never done, May told herself. Weed a bed and turn round and the weeds are sprouting again behind your back. She had plenty to occupy her for the rest of the day.

She visited Grant Wheatley in his study, which was coming to resemble a cross between an ultra-modern office and an electronics workshop. The visit was ostensibly to have him agree her budget for plant purchases, the employment of Work Experience helpers and re-turfing the grass where the police had spoiled its previous bowling-green perfection. In fact, her main motive was to smooth over a situation which she felt to be delicate. In the normal course of events, she owed the Wheatleys a dinner and should properly have included them with her invitation for the Sunday. On the other hand, space was at a premium and surely a meal for an employee did not call for a return invitation?

She was about to broach the subject when Grant gave her an opening. He selected a small batch of letters clipped together. 'All this fuss over the bod deddy—' (May flinched and he hid a smile) '—seems to have roused some interest. Or perhaps this is the season when visits begin? Anyway, I have some requests through the Tourist Information Office for small parties wanting guided tours of the garden. Do you usually deal with these? I can answer them for you if you want to accept them.'

'If that's all right with you.'

'No problem. It seems selfish to have such a splendid garden and not let other people enjoy it. You keep any payment of course.' (May breathed a sigh of relief. The fees and tips were an important part of her income.) 'You deserve some return for all the work and skill.'

May thanked him, partly for the concession and the compliment but also for opening up the subject for her. 'I have another party booked for tomorrow,' she said. 'A freebie. Will Largs and Bob and Jenny are coming – strictly to look at the garden. I thought they might care to look at it as a garden rather than as a murder scene. I'll give them a meal afterwards.'

'That sounds like a good idea.' Evidently Grant's mind was on other things than dinner invitations. 'May I come on the walk with you – freebie, of course? I've seen most of it on my own, obviously, and I'm bowed down with pride of possession, but I'd love to hear what you say to visitors and be able to ask penetrating questions.'

'Of course,' May said. 'Not too penetrating, I hope. You'd be welcome even if it wasn't your own garden.'

'We'll give them a drink in the house between the walk and your dinner.' Where another man might have made a pencilled note, Grant tapped a reminder into his computer. 'I saw you going off with Bob Welles,' he said. 'I assumed that you weren't having a tryst, because some of the same cars and faces started turning up again. I suppose we don't get back to our old, peaceful existence just yet. How are they getting on with their enquiries, do you know?'

'I've no idea. They aren't saying much, possibly because there isn't much to say. I suppose that, after three years, there aren't many physical clues left and people's memories are pretty hazy about who was where when and who said

118

what to whom. I think they're asking questions of absolutely everybody, hoping to ask the right one, whatever that may be, and tabulating the answers to see what shows up. But I maybe helped a bit. I found a hatchet buried in the compost from round about the right period.'

'The murder weapon – I suppose we have to call it that?'

'I suppose so. I always wondered why there wasn't one among the tools in the shed, but I never needed it. I more or less told the Sheriff that. There's a perfectly good axe I use for splitting logs.'

Grant's surprise showed in his face. 'You chop the firewood on top of everything else? For yourself and the house? Is there no end to your efforts?'

'It keeps me warm in the winter, two different ways,' May said.

'You may be getting some help shortly. What Polly said about a chauffeur made sense. I asked at the job centre, for a good driver who could also help around the house and give you a hand in the garden. It would be a relief not to have to worry about parking the car and walking back in the rain to fetch it, or about having it vandalized; and I could enjoy going out for a meal without counting my drinks,' Grant said reflectively. 'The name they offered me was that of one Colin Wilson. Do you know him?'

May thought back. 'I haven't set eyes on him for a while,' she said at last, 'but I remember him. Mrs Mellor used to get him to drive her around after her husband fell ill. He's a good driver. He doesn't drink. He's always willing but I don't think he's very strong. I seem to recall that he only has one lung. He's all right,' she added quickly. 'I wouldn't ask him to chop logs or do any heavy digging but he could help me with the light work. He lives

119

in the village and does odd jobs for people. I've never heard that he was anything but honest.'

May paused. Grant Wheatley seemed to have ample funds, indeed somebody had said that he drew a substantial share of about a quarter of the money spent on computer games and even more money from a smaller proportion of a computer system used in many of the largest organizations. He might resent any suggestion aimed at possible economies. On the other hand, her frugal soul hated to see money poured down the drain. 'You could probably hire him by the day when you wanted him.'

Grant waved the suggestion aside. 'But did you like him?'

May considered what was, after all, a very sensible question. 'I had nothing against him,' she said.

'But?'

'But we didn't have anything in common. He doesn't know much about gardening and I know damn-all about cars. If you take him on, you won't have to worry about us wasting your time gossiping.'

Grant laughed aloud. 'That's a better recommendation than many,' he said.

The day was almost gone. If May was to entertain next day, she needed some shopping. On the other hand, the guests were to be given their preprandial drinks at the Lodge. Anything else she still needed, if not to be found among supplies hoarded in the freezer against such emergencies, would be obtainable in the village. She took carrots and potatoes from their clamps in the kitchen garden.

She selected a large pheasant from the freezer and then, on mature thought, substituted two smaller ones. She

could always eat any leftovers cold, but a single pheasant
could prove disastrous if it turned out to be badly shot-up
or to have been the subject of dispute between two dogs. It
was difficult to be sure while it was still frozen in the bag.

May spent the Sunday morning trying to undertake a
number of simultaneous activities, but the sensation was
comfortably familiar to her from her experience of managing a large garden with only occasional staff. Between
preparing the pheasants and the vegetables for the evening's meal she cleaned and tidied the cottage and managed
a tour of her little domain, hoe in hand and checking that
all was immaculate, no weeds in view and no plants wilting
from thirst. She picked up a few scraps of paper which had
blown from the direction of the village and noted down
some tasks for the coming weeks.

Back in the cottage, she decided that neither the dress
that she had worn at the dinner party nor the one that she
had worn for the inquest hit quite the right note. The trunk
containing Janet Mellor's clothes had been brought down
from the attic at the Lodge by the combined teamwork of
the staff, assisted and directed by Grant Wheatley, and
conveyed to May's cottage on the trolley which was kept
for such purposes. The trunk now occupied much-needed
space on the floor of her bedroom, where it caught her toes
or her shin whenever she made the least careless movement. Trying on and then putting aside the most suitable
choice of dress, she hung some of the others in her wardrobe. The remainder would have to await the attention of
her iron.

Beneath a sombre dress, which she supposed had been
reserved for funerals, there was a layer of underwear. She
deferred for later consideration the question of whether she

would care to inherit another woman's lingerie, some of it so frivolous that she was sure that Mrs Mellor could never have given it the seal of her approval. The trunk, empty or not, could be trolleyed back to the Lodge later and somebody else could decide whether to return it to Mrs Mellor.

By mid-afternoon she had pressed the dress, removed the ironing board from her dining table and laid the table for four, dashed up to the Lodge to borrow wine glasses and made another visit to the garden, this time for flowers. She rarely took flowers from the garden into her cottage, partly because, strictly speaking, they were not her flowers but also because she liked flowers too much to enjoy bringing their short lives to a premature end. No flower had ever bitten her or spoken to her unkindly. She liked them better where they were. But guests expected to see flowers on the table, especially a gardener's table. She chose carefully from where her selection would not leave noticeable gaps nor spoil shape for the following year. She was rather short of vases – her mother held that you could never have too many and, holding to that principle, refused to part with any. From a heterogeneous collection under the sink May chose an Ovaltine jar that she had once painted a terracotta colour. In it, she arranged Japonica and some white lilac. With aubretia and alyssum trailing down the sides, nobody would notice the pot.

Occupying more than its share of her tiny kitchen space was the chest freezer, bequeathed from the Lodge when Mrs Mellor had re-equipped. Pheasants, trout and other fruits of the wild took up much of the interior, at that time of year. She considered making an apple crumble from the contents of one of the bags of stewed apples from the previous autumn. Instead, in an outburst of extravagance, she chose an almost forgotten cheesecake for the sweet course and left it to defrost.

The sun had gone off the greenhouses as the shadows of the big beeches moved across the garden. She made her evening round early, watering the host of cuttings and seedlings with unusual haste and, with an almost sybaritic feeling of guilt, making use of the hose instead of the watering cans whose contents had by now arrived at the ambient temperature. It was a tough old world outside and the seedlings had better get used to it.

Back in the cottage, she switched on the oven, fed Ellery and then it was time to make ready. Her hands, and especially her nails, again took up more than their fair share of her time. She showered and dressed with care. For years, she had lived her life without giving much thought to her appearance, but with a sense of shock she realized that she was, for the second time in a week, turning herself out at her best – an effort which she had been making at the most once a year. This, she told herself firmly as she applied a trace of make-up, was because she was receiving guests and not for the benefit of any one of them.

She was as ready as she would ever be when the sound of a vehicle drew her outside. The big four-by-four was pulling up outside the Lodge with Jenny Welles at the wheel. Grant and Polly Wheatley were already at the door of the house. May picked up a lead, called Ellery and hurried to join them.

She was spared the need to make small talk. She greeted her guests and gave Will the promised chart, which he stowed carefully in the car. Grant was studying a climbing hydrangea, which stood in a sheltered suntrap beside the front door. 'When I first saw the house,' he said, 'this was in full flower. A marvellous blue. I think it was the memory of that blue which made me sit up and take notice when the house came on the market.'

'I've got one just like it,' Will Largs said. 'You've seen it, May. But mine only flowers pale pink.'

'Dissolve a little alum in the water,' May said, 'or fork some in around the roots.' The tour was already launched. She had no need to lead the visitors around. The party conducted itself around the garden, making the small sounds of pleasure that May preferred over polite adulation. The garden seemed to have made a special effort, every blossom on tiptoe and demanding admiration. The grass walks were springy underfoot and the scents of the season made the other senses sit up and take notice. May only had to follow and answer questions. Progress was slowed by Jenny's scrupulous photography of every changing aspect.

Bob breathed a sigh which could only have been of relaxation. 'The garden looks quite different when you're not forced to wonder what horrors happened in it. I honestly never realized just how much beauty you'd managed to create here, May. You and God between you.'

'I thought you didn't believe in a personal God,' Jenny said.

'Give me another hour or two and I may come around.'

At one bed, still flaming with japonica in full flower, Polly paused and sighed. 'It's a shame that it's so far from the house.'

'They can't all be under the windows,' Grant said.

'They're supposed to tempt you to come out and walk during the better weather,' May said with mock severity. 'I've been moving things around and putting the plants which give colour in the winter where you can see them from the windows.'

'Good idea,' Grant said. 'Polly, we'll have to walk round more often.'

'I see it more than you do,' his wife pointed out. 'You take root in front of your computer and you wouldn't know it was Christmas if I didn't put on my red dressing gown and come down the chimney.'

Grant held up his hands in a gesture of surrender. 'I swear that I'll turn over a new leaf.'

'Fat chance!'

'My garden's a desert in the winter,' Will said. His own woes seemed to be taking precedence over pleasure in the Cannaluke Lodge garden. 'I have some winter jasmine. When I asked the garden centre what else I could get for winter colour, they offered me red dogwood and Christmas roses and then their eyes glazed over.'

May was not going to let his megrims spoil her pleasure as a hostess. 'There are plenty of others and most of them are highly scented as a bonus. Ask them to get you a *hamamelis mollis*,' she said. 'Or some of the viburnums – *placata*, perhaps, and *fragrans*. Or *chimonanthus fragrans*. I'll write you out a list. You have space at each end of your terrace.'

'Marvellous,' Will said. He brightened. He seemed to be enjoying the flowers but May still sensed a discontent from him. Perhaps the case was going badly. 'You might even find room for a *lonicera fragrantissima*,' she said helpfully.

Separated from the water garden by a drift of humble forget-me-nots in brilliant blue was an undeveloped area, taken over by nettles and other weeds. 'What will you do here?' Polly asked.

'Nothing, unless you desperately want something. Very few people ever come near enough to see it. It's for the benefit of the birds. Some weed seeds and insects are a

125

small price to pay for having the songbirds and butterflies around. I add some cornflower seeds occasionally to brighten it up.'

'I noticed that we seemed to be rich in birdsong,' said Grant. They fell silent, listening. Garden birds sang melodiously. May thought that they were disputing territory or else calling for sex, but if her companions wanted to believe that they were hearing songs of happiness it would have been a shame to spoil the mood. Will seemed to be relaxing. The tired lines around his eyes were being reshaped into the hint of a smile.

May enjoyed her own secret smile, at herself as much as at anyone. Why, she wondered, not for the first time, did people respond to the colours of flowers? She had once, in a public park, happened suddenly on a scene where petals made a scattered carpet on the grass. Her pleasure had lasted until she came close enough to see that the petals were in reality the torn-up fragments of a magazine. She had hurried away from the sight. It still puzzled her that appreciation of a splash of colour could be switched on or off by knowledge of the colour's origin. One of her favourite roses, for instance, was the colour of blood. Why should the rose give her pleasure and the sight of blood make her feel faint? It was inexplicable but it was a fact and perhaps it was one of nature's kindnesses.

The party moved on. A mood of quiet contentment was developing. Will was opening up again and May basked in his pleasure. The water garden was duly admired. Above it, a retaining wall of dry stones, bright with tumbling rock plants, held back the first terrace – a bed of rose bushes which, heavily pruned in March, were shooting again. May put Ellery on the lead. 'I have to restrain her here,' she said. 'She's taken it into her head to dig between the roses, always in the same place.'

'Have you been using bonemeal as a fertilizer?' Will asked. 'Or dried blood?'

'Neither of those.' The others were looking at her. The joy seemed to be dying out of a perfect afternoon. 'Oh, come on!' she said. 'We're here to look at a garden, not to think about . . .'

'Bod deddies?' Jenny suggested.

'Please,' May said. 'Let me live down my humiliation. Just because my dog wants to dig there doesn't mean anything. She probably buried a bone.'

'Or somebody else did. Think about it, May,' Bob said. 'Dogs have an unbelievable sense of smell, something like a million times more sensitive than ours, or so one of our handlers told me. Your dog saw a whole lot of people getting excited around a hole in the ground where she could have detected a scent too faint for our less developed senses. If she smelled a similar scent elsewhere in the garden, wouldn't that make her want to dig? That, in embryo, is how spaniels are trained to find drugs or explosives. Or bod – er – bodies.'

The sun still shone but May felt a shiver. 'Probably a dead mole,' she said stubbornly. 'Or Joe Scott might have seized the opportunity to dispose of any kind of dead animal while they were making the bed. He was quite capable of shooting somebody's cat if it peed on his vegetables.'

'Try letting her off the lead,' Will said. 'Please.'

'She'll just scoot earth on to the path.'

'I think you'd better co-operate with the law,' Grant said. 'We'll set your Work Experience children to clearing up any mess tomorrow.'

127

'I have other things for them to do tomorrow,' May said unhappily. 'But it's your path.' She let Ellery off the lead. The spaniel looked curiously up at her and when her mistress made no move to stop her she made a leap to the top of the wall. She sniffed the earth, moved, sniffed again and then began to dig with a dedication more appropriate to a terrier. Behind May, Jenny's camera clicked and whirred.

'That's enough,' Will said suddenly. 'Call her off, please.' May attached the lead and fetched the reluctant spaniel away from the hole. 'Whatever it is,' Will said, 'we'd better have a look.'

'My job, I think,' Bob Welles said. 'We don't want to call out the team for a dead cat – we'd never be allowed to live it down. I can borrow your boots from the car?' he asked Will.

'I ought to do it,' May said. 'I can change. You're dressed.'

'That never stopped him yet,' said Jenny. 'And if . . . if there is anything there, he'll want to be able to testify that the site was kept as uncontaminated as was practicable.' She was looking drawn.

'Lend me a spade?' Bob asked May.

'Not a good one. You've still got my only good spade.'

'A bad one will do.'

'Well, I'm not having earth all over the place,' May said. 'I'll get the big tarp. Try not to damage the roots when you dig.'

'I'll come with you,' Will said. 'You don't want to spoil that dress.'

Will and May walked together in the direction of the tool shed. 'I had hoped to have you to myself,' he said.

'Is that why you've been grouchy?'

'Have I been? Perhaps that's the reason.' He lowered his voice and gave her a look that sent a warm glow through her. 'I was looking forward to whispering sweet nothings in your ear among the roses, and the party has grown into a sixsome and the occasion has become rather less than romantic. You must know that I fancy you like mad. Think how propitious our names are. I will and you may.'

May laughed in spite of the occasion and herself. 'On the other hand, I may not. Had you thought of that?' She considered changing her dress. That brought another thought to her mind. She forced herself to ask the question which had seemed too shameful to ask earlier. 'On the last occasion when we uncovered a body,' she said in a small voice, 'I fell asleep on top of my bed with the curtains open. When I woke, I was covered up. Whose kind thought was that? I haven't liked to ask around.'

'I'm flattered that you feel you can ask me. I didn't want you to catch cold. I left the curtains and the light on in the hope that you would never realize that you'd been intruded on. There's no need to blush. I tried not to peep, but I thought that you were very beautiful. That was when I realized how much more there was to you than a bright mind and a sense of humour.'

The compliment was strangely inverted but acceptable. May tried not to think about the spectacle she must have presented. 'I don't know what you must think of me,' she muttered.

'In what respect? Because you let yourself be plied with rather more wine than was good for you?' He sounded amused. 'Up here, it's considered quite normal for a man to drink himself stupid and shocking for a woman to take more than a sip of sherry. But where I come from we take a rather more sensible but liberal view. You behaved in a

129

perfectly sensible and ladylike manner, so there was no harm done.'

Caught up between indignation and shame but flattered nevertheless, she found that her voice had almost deserted her. Huskily asking Will to wait, she detoured into the cottage to leave the indignant Ellery confined. She took the opportunity to turn down the oven and switch on the rings under her vegetables at a low level. The living would still have to be fed.

In the tool shed, May stooped to the big tarpaulin but Will picked it up without undue effort and dumped it in the barrow. May made a sound of protest but he said, 'There's nothing on my suit that won't brush off. In my job, you have to get used to clothes not lasting for very long. You bring the spade, but wash it first if you will. I want to be able to say later that it was clean.' He set off with the barrow along the path. Carefully holding the spade well clear of her dress, May washed it under the garden tap and followed.

The scene was little changed except that Bob now wore a pair of heavy Wellingtons with his trousers carefully tucked inside and Jenny was loading a fresh film into her camera. The Wheatleys seemed determined not to be displaced. The three men unrolled the nylon below the retaining wall. Bob managed to dig without stepping up on to the wall.

May felt hollow. 'I don't think I want to see this after all,' she said. 'I don't want it to be what I think it is. Something keeps insisting that if I'm not here you won't find what I don't want you to find. And I've had enough of being called as a witness.'

'You're right,' Polly said. 'Let's slip away.'

May led the way to the cottage. Polly looked around and

followed her into the tiny kitchen. 'I've never been inside here before,' Polly said. 'You've got less space than you'd think from outside.'

May prodded the potatoes. They were still hard. 'The gardener before Joe had a horde of children, so the Mellors almost rebuilt the place but there was no room for extension. So he got more rooms but they're absolutely tiny. His wife must have been a genius to cater for a family from this kitchen. Of course, the freezer takes up a lot of what space there was in her day. After all that, the man took a job at the garden centre and moved away. I suppose his disloyalty was my good luck in the end.'

Polly sniffed the air. 'That does smell mouth-watering!'

'Whether or not there's a body out there, and whether it's a person or a dead fox, my guests will still have to eat and I wouldn't be showing any extra respect by letting a good meal spoil. I'd ask you to join us, but Mrs Mac would be furious if you dined out without giving her notice.'

'Mrs Mac has gone to visit her daughter and she's left us a cold meal. Grant hates cold meals but he doesn't like to tell her – she's so proud of her salads. It seems to be a custom of the house to let the staff away on Sundays.'

May's intimate little party seemed to be in danger of growing into a banquet. 'My table would only seat four,' she pointed out.

'If you think there'd be enough to go round, we could eat on our knees,' Polly said hopefully.

May bowed to what seemed to be the inevitable. 'There's enough,' she said. The two pheasants would go round. Ellery would just have to sacrifice her share in them. May was less sure of the vegetables. She opened a tin of peas to supplement the carrots. 'We could go and sit down. I can't

131

offer you anything to drink except beer or lemonade. We were invited up to the house for drinks. Will was going to bring the wine.'

'I'll pop up to the house.' Polly made for the door.

'Bring glasses,' May called after her. 'And two more wine glasses.'

'Right.'

May poked the vegetables. The potatoes were still slightly hard. She poured the water off the carrots, dealt with the peas, made gravy and put two more plates in to warm. Polly returned with a jingling carrier bag, looking solemn. 'I could see them from the front door,' she said. 'Bob's stopped digging and they seem very interested in whatever he's uncovered. I have a nasty feeling that we'll know all about it soon enough. Let's have a drink and talk very loudly about something else. Gin and tonic?'

Gin and tonic had become a rarity in May's life. 'Please,' she said. 'But drown it. My head seems to have gone soft since my student days.'

'Heads are inclined to do that. You've got to keep up your intake or you lose your immunity.'

They talked resolutely about nothing for some minutes until they heard footfalls outside. Grant came in with Jenny. In answer to the question in the eyes of May and Polly, he said, 'I'm afraid so.'

May gripped the arms of her chair. Her placid life was about to be upended again and her emotions churned – and there was nothing that she could do to prevent it.

Eight

G rant was looking grim. The corners of his mouth were turned down and his usual expression of amiable contentment had vanished. 'I wish I'd come away with you,' he said. 'Will has gone to phone from the house and Bob is covering the hole with some corrugated sheets from behind the sheds. I said they could have them, I hope that's all right by you, May. Jenny's still taking photographs. They'll join us shortly. Will said to tell you that he hasn't forgotten the wine.'

'And May's invited us to eat here,' said Polly. 'I didn't think you'd fancy a cold meal on our own with all that's going on.' Grant made a wordless sound combining agreement, surprise and pleasure. 'It's all right, is it?' Polly asked anxiously. 'If you'd be happier at home . . .'

'It's not the first dead body I've seen,' Grant said, 'and I'm not quite such a delicate flower as you seem to think. If May's quite sure that she can cope, I'm delighted.'

May felt desolate to have her fears confirmed but life had to go on – for the living. 'It will stretch. They'll have to eat,' she said dully. 'And they won't be able to do much but wait around and ask questions until the same ten thousand people arrive from Inverness or all the way from Aberdeen and trample all over everything, which is going to take some time to organize on a Sunday evening. I'm

133

glad we managed to tour the garden before it gets even more messed up. Grant, would you carve the pheasants, please?'

'Surely.'

May got up and Grant followed her into the kitchen. They had to squeeze past each other as May produced the pheasants, dishes and her carving knife and poured the water off the vegetables. Polly looked in with a whisky for her husband but there was no room for her to join them. 'So tell us,' she said through the doorway.

'Not much to tell,' Grant said. 'You're sure you want to hear? What I saw was pretty much what May told the inquest about the other one. Clothing. One bone sticking out. Not very significant on their own but taken together very unpleasant. Don't think about it.'

It was good advice but there was one thing May wanted to know. She was still hoping against hope. 'Is it a man or a woman?'

'Impossible to say. But, from what shreds of clothing were still recognizable, unless it was a man who wore printed shirts, I'd guess a woman.' He gave a shiver. 'I'm not as familiar with the aftermath of death as those two are, and when you see it for real it's quite different from seeing the same sort of thing in a film. It was not my idea of pleasant viewing on an otherwise delightful afternoon! Let's not talk any more about it until we have to.' He took a sip of his whisky and went back to carving.

Bob arrived, closely followed by Jenny. Bob had changed back into shoes. His muddy hands showed some inflamed grazes from the rose thorns but he had managed to keep his clothes relatively clean. May showed him her bathroom and gave him a towel and some antiseptic. Will came in, looking grim but bringing wine. In the hall, he glanced up at the two split-cane rods lying along hooks near the ceiling. 'You do fish, then,' he said.

May seized her clothes brush and began to brush away the signs of his labours. She was glad to seize on a momentary escape from the inevitable. 'My father taught me to cast on the lawn before I was six. It's too early for salmon but the trout are beginning to take,' she said. 'Pay me another call some time.'

'I'll take you up on that. I still have my rods.' He escaped from May and succeeded Bob in the bathroom.

As she began to load the plates, May heard Polly enquiring who would like a drink. 'Or are you on duty?' she asked.

'I'm not on duty,' Jenny said. 'I'm unofficial. I'm driving, but I'll be amazed if we get on the road before morning. I'll wait and have a glass of wine, maybe two.'

Will and Bob accepted a whisky apiece. 'For all anyone knows,' Will said, 'we could have started the drinks an hour ago, hardened boozers that we are. May, I'm just wondering whether to ask you to take your spaniel round the garden again.'

'You can put it out of your mind,' May said firmly, swallowing nausea. 'For a start, your dinner's ready. Then, she hasn't been showing a similar interest anywhere else. And it seems incredible that somebody else, someone we've never heard of, is also here.'

'And, of course, even if there was a whole army of corpses, you wouldn't want the garden dug up again.'

That was perfectly true but May was not going to admit it. 'I'm not having the rest of the garden dug up for rabbits that died underground of mixy or VHD,' she said.

'I'll have to trust you to let us know if Ellery starts digging anywhere else,' Will said.

'No promises,' May said lightly.

Grant had finished carving. When the plates were ready May said, 'Right. I suggest ladies at the table and gentlemen eat on their knees. Is that all right?' The two policemen still looked uneasy. May guessed that rules or convention inhibited them from eating well near the scene of a presumed murder and as guests of a potential witness. 'Listen,' she said, 'the meal's ready and it may as well be eaten. You need food and I'm sure you're not going down to the pub. Is there anything else you can usefully do until your people get here, whoever they are?'

'If you're quite sure,' Will said.

'Of course I'm sure.'

Will gave in gracefully and sat down. May usually kept the small room rather bare for the sake of an illusion of spaciousness, confining the ornaments to a few precious pieces of china from car boot sales, carefully spaced along the mantelpiece or on her coffee table. The room was transformed by the presence of such a party. The crowding made for an atmosphere of festivity and helped to cancel the grimness of the occasion.

'No, there's nothing we can usefully do except to start asking questions. And this,' Will said slowly and carefully, 'is not a yesterday's occurrence. There's nothing urgent now. We have to wait for the police surgeon.'

'And the pathologist?' Polly asked.

Will smiled without humour. 'Police surgeon first. He or she has to certify death. It's the drill. I suppose it's to be sure that the pathologist doesn't start work on somebody who's still ticking. Not much likelihood in this case, but it's the drill.' He relapsed into a dark silence.

'Questions can wait,' May said hastily, 'but the food can't. Pour the wine.'

They ate in appreciative silence. May was surprised to see that appetites had not been spoiled by the finding of bodies. If they were sensitive enough to be put off their food by a body or two, she supposed, policemen would be as thin as rakes, which they certainly were not. When hunger was at least partially satisfied, Grant spoke. 'How are the investigations going into the first case?' he asked. 'Do you have a suspect yet?'

'At this stage of a case, I don't answer questions,' Will said.

'Can't or don't?'

The question was meant in jest but Will's look became darker. 'Don't.'

'You just answered one,' May said. Will hesitated and then laughed. The moment had passed. 'I have a question you can answer,' May said. 'If, as you say, this second case is too old to be urgent, couldn't you have unfound the body for a while?'

'You're joking! How long?'

'Until later in the summer. No? I take it you'll want to dig over the whole bed, not just around the body?'

'At least.'

'Well, can you at least allow time for me to get my juniors on the job in the morning?' May picked up her last forkload of pheasant but went on, 'One of the first things I did when I started working here was to buy in the roses and plant out that bed. It's a marvellous blaze of colour in the summer and I don't want to lose it. Give me time to move the plants into the kitchen garden. They may not survive the move but they might last long enough for me to get buds for grafting or to take cuttings.' She put the now cold food into her mouth.

Will Largs stuck out his chin. May thought madly that

he was about to read her the Riot Act and fire over her head, but Grant spoke quickly. 'Surely,' he said, 'we'd be quicker to buy new plants?'

May looked at him in surprise. In her world, plants were never avoidably sacrificed and were only purchased in order to acquire new varieties, after which they were propagated onward and lovingly preserved. Such carefree extravagance was alien. 'I suppose so,' she said at last.

'Put them on order, then. Order the snowball tree and the clematis at the same time.'

May still looked dissatisfied.

'We'll have to sift all the earth off the roots of the roses, just in case the culprit obligingly dropped his visiting card,' Will said reasonably. 'I don't think they'd survive that, not at this time of year.'

At least, May thought, he understood. She got up to clear the plates and serve the cheesecake. When she was seated again, Will said, 'We still have to establish whether or not it's the Mellor girl, but we can make that assumption for the moment. May, you came to work here shortly after she was supposed to have run off and you put the roses there. What had been planted there before?'

May could see where logic was leading them and she did not like it, but there was no alternative to honest answering. 'Nothing,' she said. 'The Mellors had been consulting me for years about the shape and design of the garden. It used to have about as much interest as a municipal grave-yard and I was trying for a more natural look. There were some suitable stones and a heap of good topsoil left over from making the water garden. I pointed out that there was room to bring the steps a few yards further down the slope, build the wall and fill in behind it with the topsoil to make another terrace bed, killing several birds with one

stone. At that stage, it would have been easy . . .' She
faltered. She had a mental picture of the drystone wall,
newly built, with space behind and somebody approaching, carrying a lightweight body in a printed dress.

'Don't go on. I take the point,' Will said.

'Thank you. That much had been done and the soil was
in place when I came here. If you look in the diary, you'll
see that I spent some of my first few weeks buying and
putting in roses and rock plants.' She paused and then
rushed on. 'If you look in the last of Joe's diaries—'

'We'll see what shape the place was in when Miss Mellor
was last seen,' Will said. 'I hadn't missed the point. Would
you happen to know who her dentist was?'

'The same as mine. I met her in the waiting room once.
Mr Walkinshaw,' May said. She swallowed a sudden
excess of saliva. 'Tell me one thing. Was the body wearing
a watch?'

'No. Why?'

'Janet Mellor was never without her watch. It was a very
good watch, rather large for a lady's watch but her near
vision wasn't too good and she didn't like wearing glasses –
she thought that, in time, they altered the shape of the
wearer's face. Has my face changed?' she asked anxiously.

'If so, it's been for the better,' Will said. May saw Polly
hide a smile.

'If it should turn out to be a woman and it isn't Janet,
you could check up on Daisy Hutchinson,' May suggested.
'She was another who ran off.'

'Good God!' Jenny said. 'How many more?'

'I don't think any,' May said. 'Mrs Ross, at the pub, said
that she's been getting Christmas cards from Daisy, but it
just seemed better to mention it now.'

'Quite right,' Will said. 'But I'll tell you this much.

Before we had a positive identification of Joe Scott, we checked the list of persons reported missing in the Region over the relevant period. There were eight. But,' he added quickly, 'five of them have returned home, properly ashamed of themselves, and another one was in deep trouble and is believed to be on the Costa del Crime. Mrs Hutchinson is back with her husband. I don't think that we'll end up bulldozing the whole garden in search of them.'

'I should hope not!' May exclaimed. 'Or you'd have to add me to the list of the missing.'

Will seemed to brighten, but before he could make a riposte he stiffened. There was the sound of a vehicle outside. The two policemen got to their feet. 'I'm sorry to break up the party,' Will said, 'but duty calls. Thank you for an interesting tour and a truly delicious meal.'

'I think he's said it all, for the three of us,' Bob said.

'I echo that,' Jenny said as the door closed behind them. 'When the dust settles, you'll all have to come to us. I just hope that I can match your standard of cuisine.'

'I'm only sorry we were so cramped,' May said.

'My dear, you'll be just as cramped with us. Bob and I live in two small flats. One of them is mostly given over to my photography but it does provide a spare bedroom for visitors. I'd better go and do my thing.' She winked. 'The more photographs I take, the better I'm paid.'

May went out with her. The daylight was almost gone. Already there were lamps at the new excavation, flashing and dimming as figures moved around them. Two more vehicles approached the Lodge.

May went back into the cottage. She allowed the spaniel to join the company. 'I didn't offer anybody coffee,' she said.

The Wheatleys were nursing small glasses. 'Don't bother for our sakes,' Grant said. 'Polly brought the remains of a bottle of brandy when she came down. Can I offer you a tot?'

'Thank you,' May said, 'but no. Your dinner taught me that any head that I ever had for alcohol is long gone. There's still a drop of wine left in the bottle. I'll stay with that.' The washing-up was calling, but it could wait. There was almost a full glass left. 'Perhaps I should go out and try to limit the damage they do. If they can put a tape round a crime scene to keep people out, I don't see why I can't put a tape round to keep them inside.'

Grant got up, led her firmly to a chair and made her sit. With the other visitors gone, there was easy-chair seating to go round. May settled down and tried to relax. She seemed to have been on her feet for days. Grant topped up her glass of wine with what was left in the bottle. 'Let it go, May,' he said. 'You won't deflect them and you do too much already. You're more upset about the rose bed than we are, but damage can be repaired. It won't be your fault or your responsibility. Polly and I can wait for it to come back to its best.'

'We can indeed,' Polly said. 'It'll make something to look forward to. Like May said, I'm just glad that we saw the garden before.'

'Before I started the whole business? I wish I'd kept my stupid mouth shut now about the *sequoia*.' May could hear her own voice beginning to disintegrate.

'If you'd done that, we'd have had a towering monster putting the house in darkness and Joe Scott and somebody else would have lain in unmarked graves,' Grant pointed out. He was tugging gently at the spaniel's ears. 'I'm more concerned about the visitors who want the guided tour. Shall I write and put them off?'

'It's the macabre side of it that's attracting them,' Polly said. 'Tell them that the price of the guided tour has gone up to . . . What do you usually take, May?'

'I usually charge two pounds, but they often give me a fiver for the couple.'

'Tell them that it's gone up to ten pounds a head while the police are here. I bet they'll pay it.'

May was horrified. 'Put them off until the fuss has died down. Please. I wouldn't want to show a lot of ghouls around and be asked morbid questions.' It was all getting a bit much and May had finished her wine. She jumped up and began to clear the table.

Polly jumped up too. 'You've done quite enough for today,' she said. 'Sit down again and I'll wash up. Grant can dry. It'll be just like it used to be.'

The unaccustomed kindness was almost the last straw. May went into her miniature bathroom and washed her face in hot and then in cold water. She sat on the lavatory pan while she composed herself. When she came out, she had herself under control. The Wheatleys were preparing for departure. May thought that they had removed the bottles along with the glasses but later she found the half-full whisky, gin and brandy bottles in her cupboard. Her crockery and cutlery had been washed without any breakages.

'An excellent meal,' Grant said. 'Our thanks.'

'And it was never boring,' said Polly. 'You certainly provide entertainment for your guests. Are you and Will becoming an item?' May had been pondering the same question, so she uttered an indignant denial. 'You could do much worse,' Polly went on. 'Of course, he's not very handsome, but looks aren't everything.'

May refused to rise to the bait. She showed them out

and then spent some time on quite unnecessary tidying of the cottage. She took one look outside and then tried not to think about what was happening to her beloved garden. At last she decided that she was tired. She went to bed, being very careful to close the curtains properly, and lay for a long time before sleep would come.

The new day was overcast, which suited May very well. A gardener can have too much sunshine. She had it in mind to get the pansy seedlings, sown under glass the previous autumn, planted out around the hole for the new tree. But, although the second body had been removed, her young helpers seemed to be fascinated by the activities of the police around the site of the fresh discovery. In desperation, she transferred them to the kitchen garden where they could plant out the last of the vegetable seedlings and hoe between the rows without the distraction of seeing what was going on beyond the garden walls.

The police were digging over the rose bed. The rose plants, with their roots carefully denuded of earth, were lying in a careless heap nearby, dying. May experienced sympathetic pangs of thirst. The rock plants also were being treated with less than due consideration. Rather than witness all this official vandalism, May spent the day in the kitchen garden. There she could keep an eye on the youngsters while spraying the espalier fruit trees with her own mixture of fungicide and foliar feed and adjusting their fastenings until they were as elegantly displayed as a floral arrangement at a wedding. She looked at the finished result with satisfaction. There was no horticultural reason for such attention to aesthetics; but beauty, she felt, is nine tenths of the object of a garden, even among the fruit. It was going to be a good year for plums.

143

Mrs Mac fed the three of them at lunchtime, but the conversation was kept firmly away from death and burial. The two youngsters had worked well. Wood pigeon had decided that the kitchen garden was a ready-made restaurant and were sitting in the trees, only waiting for the departure of their human hosts before dropping in. May had a ready-made hide in a corner, conveniently close to the brassicas. When their time came to leave, the helpers saw May preparing to lie in wait for the pigeon and demanded to be let in on the fun.

May looked at her watch. 'All right, but you're on your own time.'

'Of course.'

After a few minutes of instruction, they settled down in the hide. The girl in particular turned out to be a very good shot with May's air rifle. They left with a brace of pigeon each for their mothers to prepare and cook. Preparing a dozen pigeon for the freezer partly filled May's evening.

On the Tuesday, as for several days thereafter, the young helpers were inescapably required at school. This was rather to May's relief. Dark clouds were building and she had no wish to pay over Grant Wheatley's money to them for sitting in the shed, or to create imaginary jobs for them in one of the greenhouses. Work seemed to have finished on the ruined rose bed but a uniformed constable shooed her away from the area. She took a good look at the grass around the bed where the *sequoia* had once loomed and decided to postpone any decision about re-turfing, reseeding or re-laying there and at the new site, until after the expected rain had done its best to repair the damage inflicted by constabulary feet and tyres.

By this time, the ladies and gentlemen of the media had

heard about this find and, while a single buried body had roused in them a certain interest, the discovery of a second corpse within the same garden brought them to frenzy. Speculation about a serial killer was rife. May, for her part, tried not to consider the possibility. The two bodies could be presumed to date from some three years earlier. All the same, she was no longer quite at ease around the garden when nobody else was in sight though the presence of Ellery, who had caught her mood and barked at a blowing leaf, lent her some confidence. She locked her doors carefully at night and left a substantial mallet handy.

The police eventually gave up attempts to hold the media at bay. The Lodge was almost in a state of siege. May managed to hide away, but it was not the time of year for the greenhouses to require much of her attention. She spent a useful hour oiling and sharpening the tools and machinery in the shed. By that time, the black clouds were overhead. the rain began with a few heavy drops and gusts of wind and soon it was sheeting down, whisking around corners, bouncing off the paths and forming puddles even on the grass. There was a distant clap of thunder.

At least the rain had driven the reporters indoors or perhaps back under their stones. May ran for the cottage. The deluge was set to continue at least until daylight was gone, so replacement of any seedlings damaged by the downpour would have to wait until morning. May locked the doors. She phoned the garden centre to reserve some plants; and Charlie Mostyn to order another load of dung. Then, for once, she felt that duty was done and she was free to indulge in an early bath and to put on a comparatively respectable dress. As a further sop to her own morale, she even put on a touch of make-up and spent some minutes brushing out her hair.

For this she was thankful when, just as she finished catching up with her laundry chores, there was a knock at the door. May peeped cautiously out of the sitting-room window but it was not the killer returned for a third victim. May drew back two bolts, removed the chain and unlocked the door to admit Jenny Welles.

'There's a media circus going on up at the house,' Jenny said. She left a hooded raincoat to drip in May's tiny porch but brought a big camera bag into the sitting room. 'I couldn't face it. Bob's having to hold a press conference and talking as much as possible without actually saying anything. He's coming to you with some questions when he can get away, so I thought I might come and visit with you until he arrives. Is that all right?'

May found herself smiling warmly. She liked Jenny. 'Yes, of course. I'm glad of the company. I hate thunder. I know that statistically a man is ten times as likely to be struck by lightning as a woman is, but that's only because there are more men out of doors at any one time than women. If somebody cared to take the survey further they'd probably find that women gardeners are an exception. That thought always leaves me with the idea that thunderclouds are following me around, waiting to strike. Would you like a drink?'

'A cup of tea would go down a treat.' From the bag, Jenny produced a soft cloth and began drying invisible dampness off an expensive-looking camera.

May put on the kettle and prepared a tray. Through the open door she said, 'I hope the police pay you well for all this work.'

'I lose money on it,' Jenny said. 'I used to do very nicely, freelancing; but any shots I take of a case I've photographed for the police I can't sell until the case is over, by which time nobody's quite so interested. That's the agreement and I'm stuck with it, but I can't let Bob down when there isn't a police photographer available in a hurry. They're short-handed just now. Some soft porn photographs were turning up on the Internet and somebody recognized the interior of a police garage. Heads rolled.'

'I can see how they might,' May said.

The kettle came to the boil. May made tea, carried the tray through and joined Jenny on the settee. Jenny had finished with her camera and was checking a formidable telephoto lens. She put the lens away and accepted a scone.

'How are Bob and Will getting on with their investigations? Or aren't you allowed to spill the beans?' May enquired.

'I asked Bob whether it would matter. He said I don't know anything he wasn't going to tell you when he comes. The only big news is that they've confirmed that it's Janet Mellor's body.'

'I don't think there was ever much doubt of that,' May said. She looked out of the window at the rain and the darkened sky. 'It's very sad to have it confirmed, all the same. Life should have been about to become a glorious picnic for her.'

Jenny looked at her curiously. 'Is life a picnic for you?' she asked.

May shrugged. 'I'm not a picnic sort of person. Mrs Mellor will be heartbroken. She always hoped that Janet would walk back in some day, with a ring on her finger and a couple of grandchildren in tow. But I suppose—'

May was interrupted by a brilliant flash. She jumped, but the clap of thunder never followed. Jenny was lowering a camera. 'What was that for? To sell to the papers?' May asked. '"Witness who found body now raped and strangled"?'

'I promise I won't let the media have it without asking you first.'

'You could hardly ask me first if I'd been raped and strangled.'

They laughed. Jenny whipped up the camera and took another shot. 'That's good,' she said. 'One laughing and one sad and soulful.'

'But what do you want them *for*?'

Jenny took a third shot. 'Lost and puzzled. I'm the last person to judge another woman's looks,' she said, 'but men seem to find you attractive.'

May laughed again and got another flash. Her eyes took a second to recover. 'What rubbish!' she said. 'Really, why are you snapping me?'

'Library shots,' Jenny said. 'Just in case.'

'Rubbish again. Or do the police suspect me of having done away with Joe in order to steal his job? You know damn well I'm never going to figure in a *cause célèbre*.'

'I'm thinking of transferring your head on to a more busty nude body and selling it to a porn magazine.'

May turned away and poured tea. 'Jenny,' she said, 'I am losing patience. If my image is going beyond my control I want to know where and what for.'

'Somebody asked me. That's all I'm prepared to say.'

'The police? They want a mugshot of me to show around?'

Jenny was chuckling. 'Of course not.'

'Don't tell me that Bob wants a photograph of me to keep under his pillow!'

Jenny stopped laughing. 'Not Bob. Damn!' she added. 'I've said too much.'

Belatedly, the penny dropped and with it May's jaw. 'Will Largs? Will wants photographs of me?'

'No. Well, yes. Don't let on that I told you. He's very taken with you, but you knew that.'

'I knew nothing of the sort,' May said indignantly.

Jenny looked at her doubtfully, as though at an untruthful child. 'You must have done, everyone else did. The other day, he said that you were the only woman alive who could take a drink and still talk sense.'

'He probably meant get thoroughly sloshed and still talk his ear off.'

'Quite likely. The only question is, what do you think about him?'

May had been aware of a warm sense of pleasure when Will was around and of disappointment when the police presence failed to include him, but she was not going to admit it. Any such tenderness was a delicate seedling, too frail to withstand direct sunlight. She could feel her colour rising. 'I think he's very nice,' she said.

'I bet that's the first time anybody's ever called him nice,' Jenny said. There was a new animation in her face and a spark in her eyes. Was every woman for miles around, May wondered, a confirmed matchmaker? 'Come on, May. What do you really think?'

'I think you've got the wrong end of the stick,' May said hotly. 'I don't think he's "taken" with me, as you so delicately put it. I think he may fancy my little pink body. That evening of the Wheatleys' dinner party, when I'd had two or three glasses of wine—'

'Or four or five,' Jenny said.

'Whatever. I was desperately sleepy. I dropped my clothes on the floor and just flopped on top of the bed, leaving the curtains open and the light on. I meant to roll

149

over, taking the quilt with me, but my memory insists that I fell asleep before I could do it. When I woke up, somebody had flipped the other side of the quilt over me. When I asked him, Will admitted that he'd come in and covered me up.' May decided not to mention, nor even to remember, such matters as her trainers still on her feet and her jeans around her ankles.

'There you are, then,' Jenny said triumphantly. 'If he'd only fancied your pink body, there was his chance. He's said twice that he thinks you're intelligent and once he remarked that he likes your sense of humour. He also said that you're the only woman he's seen in trousers who didn't look fat-bummed. I could have hit him. I wear trousers most of the time when I'm working. I have to climb over all sorts of things with fat coppers trying to look up my skirt.'

May wanted to believe what she was hearing about Will and herself, but it all seemed far-fetched. 'Your bum doesn't look fat,' she said. 'Anyway, men like a bit of bum on a woman, or so one of them told me. You've got to be wrong. When we're together, he'll sometimes act as if he wants to run away. Next moment, he's trying to talk me into bed but not sounding as though he really meant it. He doesn't make himself very clear and he could be joking in a flirtatious way.'

'Some people talk about sex as an alternative to being witty,' Jenny said. 'But not Will.'

'It could be some sort of test of my virtue or something damn silly. But wanting photographs of me makes him sound like a lovelorn teenager.'

Jenny was nodding and smiling with a maternal tolerance that made May want to slap her. 'He can be very shy about women,' Jenny said. 'I think he always was and his marriage to a totally selfish bitch made him a dozen times worse. He's only just come round to accepting me and I've known him for years. In his work, he acts the ogre and most of his men are terrified of him. In time, they come to realize that he's training them and carrying the can for them and fighting for their promotions.

'When he's interviewing suspects, he'll chew up anybody he suspects of a crime, male or female, and spit out the pieces, but he leaves the interviewing of the more respectable female witnesses to others, usually Bob. God knows I've complained – the last thing I want is for my husband to be regularly pushed up against women who may feel a need to ingratiate themselves with the fuzz. One of these days, he might feel in the mood for a little ingratiation. But Will really does have the proverbial heart of gold. I think he only does the job because he's so indignant about the things people can do to each other. I'll tell you this, May – I've never known him sing the praises of any other woman.'

That seemed to be quite enough on that subject. 'You could have let me tidy my hair before taking photographs,' May said.

'It looks all right. Natural. I wish mine had waves like that. And I have to keep mine short in case it blows in front of the lens.'

For some minutes, Jenny tried to drag the conversation back to Will Largs and May struggled to avoid the subject. To May's relief, there was a knock at the door and she got up to admit Bob. He left an enormous golf umbrella dripping in the porch and joined his wife on the settee.

May fetched another cup and took one of the easy chairs. 'I thought policemen always went around in pairs,' she said. 'Like bookends. Or is Jenny here as your witness?'

151

'I haven't come to take a formal statement yet, just to see what background you can give us. Jenny told you that the body has been identified as Janet Mellor?'

'Yes. Not,' May said, 'that there was ever much doubt about it.'

'I suppose not. The FAI will be on Friday, but you won't be called this time. Just for background, what can you tell us about Miss Mellor? For a start, can you suggest any link between them other than this place and garden? Any person who had any kind of relationship with both of them?'

'Off the top of the head, only me,' May said. 'But I didn't exactly form a connection.'

'You, then,' Bob said. 'What else can you tell us about her?'

May concentrated. She barely noticed the occasional flash from Jenny's camera. 'I remember when she was born. I was about eight. She was an only child and she'd been a late baby – her mother must have been nearly forty at the time and her father considerably more. She was a pretty girl. You couldn't fault any of her features and they added up to one of those piquant faces that don't get forgotten easily. She played a lot of tennis, which didn't do her figure any harm. You must have seen photographs of her, but I have one or two more if you're interested.'

Bob looked surprised. 'Yes, of course we're interested. At this stage, no scrap of information is wasted.'

May got up again and fetched three albums of transparent pockets. 'These are my records of the garden, but people keep turning up in them because, really, a garden isn't a garden without people. I have an old Zeiss Ikon,' she explained to Jenny.

'A good camera in its day,' Jenny said. 'Brilliant lenses.'

Down the Garden Path

May had flicked through one of the albums. She extracted a colour print. 'This must have been taken the year she disappeared,' she said. 'I asked her to stand between the laburnums to give an idea of the scale.'

Bob glanced at the photograph and laid it aside. 'May I look through your albums? Go on talking about Janet Mellor.'

May handed over her albums, first opening one of them and finding a place. 'Each one has the date it was taken on the back. This is where Cannaluke Lodge begins. I made a record of how it was when the Mellors first asked me for advice,' she said. 'Being an only child and a late one, Janet was the apple of the Mellors' eye. She wasn't spoiled, though she very easily could have been; but they were very protective, which I honestly believe is hardly ever the best upbringing. At one time, she talked to me freely whenever I came over to advise Joe Scott, and when she could catch me alone.'

'Talked about what?' Bob asked without looking up from the photographs.

'About the things girls do talk about. Clothes and boys. And sex. I didn't think that it was my place to fill her in about the facts of life, but her mother had tried to keep her innocent, which also means ignorant, and ignorance can be dangerous. In any other area of human activity, wisdom is handed down from generation to generation but when it comes to sex they're often left to find it all out for themselves anyway and they can get the wrong end of the stick.'

Bob hid a smile. 'Very true,' he said.

'Yes. So I tried to drop a word of caution now and again. Not that it did any good. She became rather secretive. I mentioned to you once that I thought she might have had a secret boyfriend.'

153

'So you did.'

'Well, don't take my word for it,' May said. 'I have no
personal knowledge. If you want what you call "best
evidence", speak to Mrs Ross at the Firthview Inn. Or
to Margaret Ferrier. She lives in the village, in the house
with the pornographic topiary in front of it.'

Jenny Welles had been half-listening but now she
pricked up her ears and made an unconscious gesture with
her camera. 'No!' she said. 'Really? Erotic hedge trimming?
That could be worth a visit. You're sure?'

'Not what you'd call absolutely sure,' May admitted.
'She says that it's a pair of dolphins playing among waves,
but from some angles it looks very much like a couple
behaving in a most unusual manner. And nobody else
bothers to put up house numbers around there but she has
a conspicuous sixty-nine over the front door. Anyway, Mrs
Ross said that she'd seen Janet ducking up a side street in
Bonar Bridge when her mother thought that she'd gone in
the other direction and Mrs Ferrier had also seen her. That
may be how the rumours started.'

A reporter, more enterprising than the rest or better
equipped with waterproofs, came knocking at the door.
Bob got up to deal with him. The reporter was in search of
the Miss Forsyth who had given evidence at the previous
FAI. Bob sent him away with a flea in his ear.

When they had settled down again, Bob resumed his
study of the photographs. 'Who's this?' he asked.

May looked. 'That's Charlie Mostyn, the farmer.'

'The one who should have pulled the tree down?'

'That's the one.'

Bob turned over the pages. 'These give a much clearer
picture of how the garden was at the crucial times than any
amount of verbal descriptions. I'll borrow your negatives,

if I may. I'll get prints made and let you have your albums back in a day or two.' He held up an album, open, so that May could see a particular print. 'In this one, featuring Janet Mellor, I see that she was wearing a dress exactly like the one you had on at the FAI.'

'It's the same dress,' Janet explained. 'A trunk of her clothes was left at the Lodge. Polly Wheatley asked Mrs Mellor what she should do with it and Mrs Mellor said that she didn't want to see it again and to give it to me, or to charity. Same thing,' May added wryly. 'I still have it here.'

'Show me.'

Jenny swapped her camera for a smaller, digital one from her bag and the trio squeezed into May's bedroom. May threw open her wardrobe. 'Those that I've unpacked are hanging in here. There are still one or two in the trunk and some odds and ends in the bottom. And now,' she said gloomily, 'I suppose they'll all be taken away for forensic study and I shan't get them back again for years, if ever.'

'I think we can do better by you than that,' Bob said. 'Let me use your phone and I'll get a SOCO here straight away. He'll tape or vacuum the clothes for contact traces – a total waste of time after these years, but it has to be done. Any clothes that show stains may have to be removed, I don't know for how long.'

He hurried through to the phone in the sitting room. May looked at Jenny. 'Stains?' she said. 'There couldn't be any bloodstains, could there?'

'I wouldn't worry about it,' Jenny said.

'God!' May had suddenly realized where Bob's mind was going. 'That's horrible.'

Bob returned almost immediately, pulling on a pair of very thin gloves. He lifted out the last dress and the underwear and laid it on the bed. Two pairs of shoes, some old tights and a small box of make-up remained. And a small diary. Bob pounced on it and riffled the pages. 'Who would "J" be?' he asked.

'Around here? Hundreds of them,' May said. 'Hundreds. And nearly all of the male ones have roving eyes and wandering hands.'

Bob flicked through the diary. 'During the few months before she disappeared,' he said, 'she seems to have had appointments with him or her at very irregular intervals. It looks like a useful lead, but "J" will probable turn out to be her Aunt Jemima.'

Bob was as good as his word and a bald man with the universal white overalls turned up not long after he and Jenny had left. May, by then, was back in her jeans and T-shirt. She showed the newcomer into her bedroom and left him alone to make use of a small vacuum cleaner, sticky tape and a strange-looking lamp. She was working her way into a stack of unread gardening magazines when he knocked on the sitting-room door. He was carrying a carefully bagged dress over his arm. 'I'm taking this,' he said.

'The others are all right?' May asked delicately.

'Perfectly.' He looked doubtfully at her. 'No semen stains, if that's what you're worrying about.'

'Thank the Lord for that.'

May locked up and bolted the door behind him. On her way to bed, she took a long look at herself in the mirror. During her teens, she had dreamed of suddenly waking up beautiful. Jenny's words had suggested that it might have come true at last, but it was still the same old face. Oh well!

Nine

The Wheatleys (or more probably Polly on their joint behalves) had decided that Grant was overdue for some of the rest and relaxation that retirement should have brought him; and also that suitably light entertainment might be obtained by attendance at the second Fatal Accident Inquiry, the day of which was approaching. May, they said, would be welcome to travel with them. May recoiled at first, thinking that to attend the FAI uninvited would smack of ghoulishness. On the other hand, she had seen no more of Will Largs, and Bob Welles only as a fleeting figure in the distance. She rather felt that, after two bodies had been unearthed thanks to the efforts of herself and her dog, she had a proprietary claim to an interest. The weather remaining wet, she would otherwise have been reduced to an unprofitable potter in the greenhouses.

That left only the question of what to wear. Clearly none of her own clothes would do justice to the occasion, but could she bear to attend in a dress once owned by the deceased? Would it be considered disrespectful to the dead, if the act should ever become public knowledge? Serious reflection while sorting seed potatoes for a late planting reminded her that the only dress showing semen stains had been removed by the police and that to spurn the others would be no more logical than to refuse the use of a bed because somebody might once have had sex in it. She picked out a cotton dress printed in autumnal colours (unsuited to the season but muted enough for an FAI) and ran the iron over it.

Grant had a minor appointment in Dornoch, which he could fit in before the FAI was due to open. The small town seemed to be fuller than ever. May had to direct Grant to park in an undeveloped industrial estate behind the court building. Her thrifty lifestyle had resulted in May having for once a bank balance which, if not exactly healthy, was at least in the black, so she indulged in a visit to a shoe shop and the purchase of two pairs of shoes. These, while tolerably comfortable, would between them 'go' acceptably well with most of the clothes inherited from the subject of the FAL.

May and Polly took their seats in the courtroom in good time and were joined by Grant as proceedings were about to open. The seating had not been made any more comfortable since May's previous visit. They had to sit through a number of remand applications and an incomprehensible legal debate about some case still to come. At the previous FAI, May had been too preoccupied and involved to pay much heed to her surroundings. She glanced around the half-panelled room without seeing much to relieve the eye. The three large portraits of formidable-looking gentlemen seemed to represent all that she found most intimidating.

The Fatal Accident Inquiry was called at last.

Will Largs was the first witness. He seemed, to May, to be both strange and yet familiar. He was not handsome but, she decided, she could settle for rugged. To her, he could never be boring; but she had heard every word that he was saying several times already. She fell into a reverie while he described the finding of the body and agreed that the finding of a second body, little more than a stone's throw from where the other had been found, either was a startling coincidence or suggested a strong connection between the two events.

At this point, May was jerked back to full attention when the Procurator Fiscal brought her own name into it. Will, however, took the digression so coolly that May decided that it had been the subject of prior agreement. He agreed that May had been present on both occasions as he had himself.

'Did Miss Forsyth seem unwilling to have the rose bed excavated?' the Procurator Fiscal asked.

'She did,' Will replied. 'But very understandably. I have here a photograph of the bed in full bloom last year. Miss Forsyth was very reluctant to have the appearance of the area sacrificed, probably for two years, on no better grounds than what at the time was, after all, no more than the expert advice of her spaniel.'

There was laughter in the room. An enlargement of one of May's photographs was passed to the Sheriff, who smiled and said, 'Understandable, as you say, Mr Largs.'

Will Largs was then withdrawn from the stand. His eyes singled out May and he gave her an almost imperceptible smile before taking a seat two rows in front of her.

The next witness was a pathologist from Inverness, a different man from the one who had testified at the previous FAI. May disliked him on sight. He had a layer of fat on a squat frame; and a close-fitting suit was not doing him any favours. His expression was supercilious. There could be no doubt that he very much enjoyed the sound of his own voice. May felt that his evidence, compelling though it was, could have been disposed of in at the most ten minutes, and by restiveness in the room it seemed that others agreed with her. But, despite some effort on the Procurator Fiscal's part to hurry him up, he described in minutest detail the body of a young woman in her late teens or early twenties. He went into even more detail than had his predecessor about the processes of decomposition which follow death and several of those present were looking green before he moved on. The condition of the body was consistent with death and burial having occurred around three years earlier. Her health, as far as could be determined after such a lapse of time, had been excellent. He had prepared a chart of the teeth from which he understood that identification had later been made.

At last, when much of his audience had been lulled almost to sleep, it was jerked into attention. The presence of a foetus indicated pregnancy at an early stage. The cause of death had been four penetrating puncture wounds, driven upward under the ribs. He had found traces of earth in the wounds, one of which had penetrated the heart. He had been shown a garden fork and from the spacing and shape of the tines could confirm that this or something very similar had been the weapon. The garden fork was produced and identified. May recognized it as having come from Cannaluke Lodge.

He then described at some length the care which had been taken to preserve any material attaching to the body or its clothing. The stir of interest was dying down and his reluctant audience was lapsing again into its torpid state before he once again made them take notice. With an air of awarding himself a special pat on the back for enterprise beyond the call of duty, he stated that he had found traces of pollen, which he had sent to the forensic science laboratory in Aberdeen. It had been referred to the University's Department of Biology. He had been informed only that morning that the pollen had been identified as rhododendron pollen, suggesting that the body had been interred in mid to late summer.

This was evidently news to the Procurator Fiscal. 'I shall be introducing evidence as to the identity of the deceased. You may not be aware,' he told the witness, 'that she vanished from her home in the month of March.'

'It is not for me to draw conclusions,' said the pathologist, 'but I suggest that burial may not have occurred until several months after her disappearance. As to when during that interval she died, the condition of the body was such that I would find it very difficult to offer an opinion.'

There was a stir of interest in the courtroom. Will Largs was sitting up very straight. The Procurator Fiscal was visibly flustered but managed to dispose of the witness without offering him the opportunity to drop any more bombshells.

At that point, May suddenly demanded a pen or pencil and a scrap of paper from Grant and was beginning to scribble a note when Will was recalled to the stand. His second testimony was brief. The dental chart had been shown to Mr Walkinshaw, a local dentist, who had identified it as pertaining to Miss Janet Mellor, a former resident in Cannaluke Lodge who had disappeared about three years previously. Mr Walkinshaw was not available to give evidence but his written and witnessed statement was offered in evidence. The police were following up certain fresh leads and requested an adjournment.

The adjournment was granted and the courtroom cleared.

May hurried to catch Will Largs only to find that he was

awaiting her in the hallway. 'I must speak to you,' May said.

Will was looking strained but he smiled and nodded. 'I can give you your photographs back. And you might be interested to see over the police station,' he said.

'I would indeed,' May said. She had a sublime confidence that anything shown to her by Will Largs would be interesting.

The Wheatleys had caught up with May. It looked as though Grant was about to say that he would enjoy being shown over the police station, but Polly gave him a quick nudge.

Will glanced at his watch. 'Lunch first, I think. You don't mind if I carry her off?' he asked Grant pointedly.

Grant fielded a quick glare from Polly. 'Of course not,' he said. 'You'll see that she gets home?'

'Yes, of course.'

The Wheatleys headed for the adjacent Castle Hotel. May found that she had been deftly detached from her employers and her afternoon planned for her. They walked under Will's umbrella the short distance to a small restaurant almost opposite the police station. There were people around, several of them having been at the FAI. May hesitated, feeling that her topic might be too confidential for discussion while others were around.

Will suffered no such constraint. 'I hope you didn't mind your name being mentioned in evidence,' he said quietly. 'I talked it over with the Procurator Fiscal beforehand and we felt that the media would certainly jump on the coincidence and start speculating about your part in the murders, hinting at the old saw about the person who finds the body being a prime suspect. It seemed better to make it clear from the start that the police see nothing significant in it.' He spoke almost absently. May could guess what was on his mind.

'I thought that it must be something like that,' she said. 'I couldn't see any other reason for it. Thank you. That was considerate.'

A waiter arrived to take their order. Will let May make her choice and then, without looking at the menu, said, 'I'll have the same.' The waiter fiddled with cutlery and then left them in peace. There was enough chatter and subdued music around them to satisfy May that she would not be overheard. 'I tried to write you a note,' she said, 'but you were called out to resume your evidence before I finished it. That pathologist got the dates wrong.'

Will leaned back in his chair and blew out a breath of relief. 'Well, thank God for that! We never treat that man's utterances as gospel, but what he said opened up what they call "a whole new can of worms".' He produced a boyish grin which transformed his face. 'I always thought that that was a stupid expression – I mean, why worms? – but when he suggested that Janet Mellor had been buried in midsummer or later I suddenly saw all the possibilities wriggling and twining together. And also the twists and turns that a defence counsel could put into whatever case we could make. So please tell me again that he was wrong.'

'Nobody was ever more wrong. He must have been thinking of the common purple rhododendron. I forget its proper name, but I think it's *rhododendron ponticum*. Joe Scott had worked on the West Coast where the rhododendron is treated almost as a weed because it grows so tall, spreads so aggressively and is so difficult to eradicate. I've been planting some of it recently because they're easily propagated, they form a good screen and they don't proliferate here the way they do when they're full in the path of the Gulf Stream. But Joe wouldn't have them. When Janet disappeared, the nearest rhododendrons to where she was found, and the only ones to windward the way the wind usually blows there, would have been *rhododendron praecox*, which flowers in March. Joe's diary and my photographs between them can prove it.'

His grin had faded as he listened but the smile came back at full strength. 'If the time ever comes, can we call you to speak to it?'

'I suppose so.'

'I'd been wondering how we could account for the missing months. If we went by what that pathologist was saying, we'd have to assume that she died several months after her departure from home. That would mean that she was hiding somewhere between when she vanished and when she was buried. So she would have had to come or be brought back to be killed. Or else that the body was kept somewhere and buried later.' He shrugged. 'We would have been asking the wrong people all the wrong questions. We could have been hunting a red herring in pursuit of a wild goose up a blind alley for months. We owe you a debt.'

'Happy to have been of service,' May said lightly, but she warmed inside.

'I mean it. You've produced the magical answer again. I think that you must be a witch,' Will said. 'Be very careful. The last witch to be burned in Scotland, the unfortunate Janet Horne – another Janet! – met her fate just outside the town and not so very long ago.'

Their starters arrived. They waited quietly until they had privacy again. 'This is all very helpful,' Will said. 'I don't think we need worry too much that a false conclusion went into the record. I'll explain to the Fiscal. The dates fit well into our current theory.'

May stopped basking in his approval and paid attention to his last few words. 'You're making progress, then?'

'If you'd asked me that question two days ago, I'd have had to say no.' He sighed and shook his head. 'It seemed that we could never find a starting point. We were asking the wrong questions, of course, but on top of that I never, ever, came across such a close-mouthed bunch. Some places, people are only too eager to tell tales about their neighbours. Elsewhere, they're more reserved. Around your neck of the woods, you'd think that they were all deaf and blind. Perhaps it's a matter of *do as you would be done by.*'

Will paused and shook his head. 'But yesterday afternoon we found the love nest in Bonar Bridge – the rented rooms where Janet Mellor used to meet her lover. From the landlady's description we were able to home in on a particular gentleman and invite him to come in for a chat. He refused to give us a sample of his DNA and then smoked a cigarette in the station, which gave us all that we needed. It had to be sent to Aberdeen but the lab, I will say, has moved with amazing despatch.' Will Largs, on the verge of saying too much, fell suddenly silent.

'And his DNA matched the foetus? And the sperm stains?' May asked helpfully.

Will gave what May interpreted as an involuntary nod. 'You said it, I didn't.'

'But you can't tell me who?'

'No. Though I dare say it will be all over your neighbourhood before you get home. Your neighbours may not talk to us but they talk to each other, without a doubt.'

The waiter returned, removed their soup plates and put their main course in front of them. Will frowned. 'Did I order this?' he demanded.

'I ordered it. You just said that you'd have the same.'
'Then I'm sure that I'll enjoy it.'

May knew that Will, now that he could again see his way clear ahead, was eager and secretly impatient to get back to work. She was usually a slow eater but she hurried the remainder of her meal. The rain had stopped and there was a drying wind. As they crossed the road to the police station – a large, red building facing the length of the principal street as though about to hold up a hand to stop the traffic – she had to lengthen her stride to keep up. She was questioned by Will in a hard, echoing interview room where May made and signed a formal statement. May was given her tour of the police station by the local Detective Constable, but it was a cursory tour which bored her. She was piqued to be dispatched homeward in the care of a young and friendly traffic policeman in a small panda car. Will, she told herself, had work to do.

If the discovery of a second buried body had caught the interest of the media, the facts emerging from the second Fatal Accident Inquiry had brought them back in strength. The police, having finished their own work, had left the household to cope as best it could. Even from a distance it could be seen that the house was under siege. If the ground had been dry or she had been in her usual working garb, May would have insisted on being dropped at the bridge, but out of consideration for the dress and her shoes she accepted a lift almost to the door of her cottage.

Several reporters had attended one or other FAI and they were around her like midges, determined to pry some exclusive details out of her. Some would have pushed after her into her cottage until she stated loudly to nobody in particular that she was about to change her clothes. Even then one woman reporter would have followed her if May had not excluded her by brute force. Emerging, May found that the only successful technique was to pretend that the individuals did not exist, walking in silence between and around them and over their feet, not acknowledging their questions by even a flicker of an eyebrow. There was no denying that they hampered her activities for the rest of the day although, conversely, she found their pestering a mild comfort. The prevailing interest was getting through to her but there was little risk of a serial killer operating under their lenses.

The last persistent reporter was dispatched by the expedient of pushing a hoe at him and inviting him to do something useful.

Next morning came in cloudy but dry, still with the good drying wind. Duke Ellon arrived to cut the grass. The reporters had not returned but May was aware of still being within the range of a distant TV camera, under the control of a director who may have been hoping against hope that she would stumble on more bodies or commit some other indiscretion.

May had some small jobs waiting which would require the hire of specialist tools from the horticultural firm and Duke had proved a reliable negotiator in the past. She was impressing the details of her requirements on him when a new-looking Audi saloon dashed up the drive and stopped with a yelp from the tyres. The driver's door opened before the car had quite halted and Margaret Ferrier came hurrying, almost running across the grass.

May had an uncomfortable feeling that she could guess what was coming but she was not to be diverted. If she could ignore a rampant reporter she could certainly expect

Margaret to wait for a few seconds. 'And I want you or Hamish to do the work,' she said. 'Not that idiot with the stripe in his hair.'

'I've got it,' Duke said.

'May—' Margaret began.

'Just a minute. I'll run over it again.'

'I've got it,' Duke said patiently, 'but I'll have the boss phone you to make sure.' He jumped back on to the machine and made his escape across the grass.

Satisfied that nothing was about to go irreparably wrong, May gave Margaret her full attention. The other woman was obviously distraught. Her hair was in disarray, unlike its usual perfect set, and she wore no make-up. May realized suddenly that she was a very plain woman who gave the impression of having passable looks by means of careful presentation.

'If you want to talk about what I think you do,' May said, 'we'd better go indoors. There's a TV van lurking and they could have all kinds of listening devices.' She led the way to her cottage and through into her bedroom. 'Maybe I've been watching too much television,' she said, 'but I believe they can listen to a conversation through glass. We're at the back here. You take the chair and I'll sit on the bed. You don't look too good. Would you like a cup of tea? Or a proper drink?'

Margaret's tongue peeped through her lips. 'I won't drink,' she said at last. 'I'll have to drive . . . back. A cup of tea, though . . .'

'Wait.' May walked the few paces to the kitchen, put on the kettle and came back. 'Now.'

'You know what's happened?'

'I'd be guessing.'

Margaret looked at her doubtfully. 'They're all saying

168

that you have a thing going with that Detective Super-intendent, Largs, or whatever his name is.'

May wondered whether a blush could be prevented by sheer force of will. 'I know the Superintendent,' she said. 'We're not a couple. He keeps coming back to me for information because I'm one of the people who knew Janet and Joe and the garden.'

At any other time, the possibility of a romance would have monopolized Margaret's attention, but she was too fraught to be diverted. After one doubtful glance she said, 'And you didn't know that Jim's been arrested? He thinks he's going to be charged with those murders.'

'No, I didn't know it. I knew that they had a suspect, that's all. I was afraid that it might be Jim as soon as I saw you coming out of your car like a rabbit with a ferret on its tail. I'm so sorry.'

Margaret made an anxious gesture. Her hands were shaking. 'They searched our house yesterday afternoon. All they found was a little bag of cannabis left over from years ago. Jim used to buy it from Joe Scott for my mother – she had multiple sclerosis and it was the only thing that helped. Joe used to grow it in the greenhouse here – did you know that?'

'I found out the other day,' May said. 'But I don't know who cured it, or where.'

'No idea. After my mother died, we forgot all about it. I don't know why the police got so het up about a little pot. They never prosecute for small quantities for personal use.'

'Perhaps they're getting excited because it suggested a connection between Jim and Joe,' May offered. 'It wouldn't exactly prove anything.'

'Maybe. But what else do they know or think they know?'

169

May could hear the kettle approaching the boil. Making tea and setting a tray gave her a respite for rapid thought. Would she be breaking a confidence if she told Margaret what Will had told her? What little she knew was surely being divulged to Jim in the course of questioning. And was it any of her business? Was she obliged to undertake the distasteful task of revealing that the other woman's husband had been unfaithful? There was no obligation, she decided as she set off with the tray, but surely it would be less of a blow to be told gently by an almost-friend rather than have the news broken through the heartless processes of law. Will might even prefer to spring the news suddenly on her in the hope of provoking some damaging admission but, if he was so cruel, May felt free to soften the blow.

'You'll have to hold your mug,' she said, 'and I'll put the tray beside me. Have a biscuit.' The other shook her head. 'When did you last eat?' May asked.

Mrs Ferrier, instead of answering, began to nibble a biscuit. Giving way to a renewed recognition of hunger she took another and while May poured the tea she almost cleared the plate. Margaret took a cautious sip of the hot tea and said, 'What can you tell me? I've got to know. They're asking our friends and neighbours questions. I must get Jim out of there. He's due to go abroad again very soon and he's freelance. If he has to call off, especially if it's because of being in the jail, they'll call on somebody else next time. If Jim loses his connections, we'll be ruined.'

May managed to make a decision. 'I don't know that I know it all, or even much of it,' she said. 'But what I do know seems damaging. And I'm afraid it's not very good news, from your point of view. You'll have to remember that this sort of thing happens all the time. I'm afraid Jim hasn't been a very good boy. The police have found a flatlet or something, where he took Janet. You knew that she was pregnant – I saw you at the Fatal Accident Inquiry. Well, I'm told that the DNA proves that it was Jim's baby.'

May broke off and waited for the tears to begin. She was ready for anything from flat disbelief to hysteria. What she did not expect was a sigh of relief and even the shadow of a smile. 'Is that all?' Margaret said.

'As far as I know. It's bad enough, surely?'

'They think that Jim killed the girl to prevent her telling me?'

'That's the only way I can look at it.'

'But I knew all along. Listen.' Margaret paused and arranged her thoughts. 'I'm sterile. I don't mean frigid. I'm a very highly sexed woman. If I'd been better looking, I could have made a killing as a call girl and loved every minute of it. But I can't have babies.

'I knew all about the rooms in Bonar Bridge. I think I used them oftener than Jim did. He was abroad so much and I could hardly have men calling here under the eyes of the neighbours. And now I've shocked you.' Margaret put her mug down. It seemed to occur to her for the first time that some explanation might be called for. 'We have an open marriage. We're both careful and, that being said, what's a little carnal pleasure between friends? Jim is away a lot and he understands that I have my needs too. We're quite frank with each other about our affairs, it's our way of making sure that they don't matter the least little bit – can you understand?'

May could not imagine ever being unfaithful to whoever it might be, but she said, 'I think so.'

'Then you'll maybe understand this. Janet Mellor fell for Jim. He told me that she said she wanted to have his baby.

The idea attracted us. It's always the way, the ones who can't have babies want them the most desperately. We met, the three of us, and thrashed it out. She wasn't visualizing herself as being permanently a mother, I think the idea of the responsibility overwhelmed her. But I think she found the idea of passion and pregnancy and childbirth very exciting. Some of her ideas may have come out of romantic novels, but that wasn't our fault.

'We're not short of money, we could well afford to stake Janet to leave home, which is what she wanted to do most of all. We could have adopted the baby and it would have had Jim's genes and we knew where the other half would have come from. Believe me, it would have worked. We were just getting ready to go and speak to her parents, who were beginning to find her a bit of a handful, and explain. When she disappeared, we thought that she'd decided that she wanted to keep the baby and had run off rather than face a battle with us. But now we find that some bastard's killed her, poor girl, and we'll have to start over again if we're going to go through with it.'

'It wouldn't be an easy defence to prove.'

Despite her worried state, Margaret managed to laugh. Already she was looking less haggard. 'That's less of a problem than you might think. We discussed it with Janet in the presence of her doctor and we've been telling friends all about it.'

They sipped tea in silence for a minute. Thinking it over, May decided that Margaret had blinded herself to another danger. 'I don't want to stir up your worries again,' May said at last, 'and I don't say that this is what happened, all I'm saying is that the police may be thinking it. Forewarned is forearmed.'

'Thinking what?'

May braced herself to deliver the blow. 'That, just as you said, Janet changed her mind about parting with the baby – threatened to keep it or to have an abortion or something – and that Jim killed her in a fit of temper and later killed Joe Scott because he found out about it.'

'God!' Margaret's expression dimmed and then brightened again. She dabbed at her eyes. 'I saw Janet the day before she disappeared – her last day alive, I suppose we have to say. She was still happy and co-operative. And I was with a friend, one of the ones we'd been discussing the whole thing with. I'd better go and make sure that she remembers and then try to see Jim and warn him.' She leaned across impulsively and kissed May's cheek. 'Thanks, May. You've been a friend, just when we needed one.'

May saw Margaret on her way. She looked after the departing Audi with compassion. Jim Ferrier had never been among her favourite people, but she liked Margaret and a prosecution for murder with all the attendant scandal would be hard on a comparatively innocent wife.

She turned away and almost collided with a man. He was undersized, with pale, protruding eyes and a pink nose. Colin Wilson had been the casual chauffeur of the Mellors and, May knew, was entering the employment of Grant Wheatley.

'Mr Wheatley said to speak to you, Miss,' he said, 'to ask if you wanted any jobs done around the garden.'

'Nothing at the moment,' May said after a moment's thought. 'Ask me again tomorrow, after I've had time to think about it. Colin, when did you start driving for the Mellors? Was it before Miss Janet disappeared?'

'Oh yes, Miss. Months before. Mr Mellor didn't trust

himself to drive after his heart went bad on him. He said he'd never forgive himself if he died suddenly at the wheel and caused an accident.'

May looked at him but he was perfectly serious. Either Mr Mellor had been joking or Colin had misquoted him. 'That would certainly be true,' she said gravely.

Colin seemed to be nursing a grievance. 'I was the last person to see her, likely,' he said, 'but the police never came to ask me.'

'They've only known about Janet for a few days. I expect they'll get around to you. How did it come about?'

Colin, it seemed, was pleased to have an audience at last. 'That last morning, Mr and Mrs Wheatley were going to Inverness so I came round to the garage to fetch their car out. Miss Janet came out of the kitchen door. She asked me if I'd seen Joe Scott. I said I hadn't. I said I could look for him if she wanted him but she said, "No way!" She said she felt like doing some weeding, it always relaxed her, she said, but she'd rather be alone.

'When we got back from Inverness, late that evening, Mrs Mellor went straight into the house, calling to Miss Janet. I came back from putting their car away and I was just unlocking my own car when Mrs Mellor came out again. She said there was no sign of Miss Janet and would I give her a call in case she was in the garden and had forgotten the time. I went around the garden, calling out, but there was no answer.'

Mention of the time in connection with Janet had started a train of thought, vague but irritating as a smell, in May's mind. 'You seem to remember very clearly,' she said.

'Aye, I do.'

'When you met Janet, was she wearing her watch?'

174

Colin's brow furrowed. 'That I couldn't say, not to swear to.'

Duke was still circulating round the lawns and grass walks. The powerful machine could cope with the grass in a single morning. In response to her wave, he halted the mower and walked to join her. The TV van seemed to have departed, but anyway what she wanted to discuss was not very confidential and she did not want Duke, who was well sprinkled with grass cuttings, inside her cottage. She led him round the back of the tool shed.

Duke, who had made more than one unsuccessful pass at her, was looking hopeful. 'Cool down,' May said. 'I'm not after you. I just want to talk where we can't be overheard from that TV van. You used to come here and help Joe when you were on Work Experience, didn't you?'

'That's right.'

Now that she had begun, May was suddenly uncertain about what she wanted to know, if indeed she wanted to know any more at all. Fumbling with words, she said, 'Did you see Janet up to the time she disappeared? How did she seem?'

Duke shrugged but he looked puzzled. 'All right,' he said. He added, 'Happy,' and then stopped. Clearly he had said it all.

'And Joe – Mr Scott – before he went missing?'

'Oh him! He was a surly bugger. Sorry, Miss Forsyth, but that's what he was. He didn't seem to get no better or no worse. After Miss Janet went missing, he didn't talk so much. But no more did anyone else.'

'I can imagine,' May said. 'How were relations between him and Mr and Mrs Mellor?'

'Relations?'

May sighed. 'How did they get on?'

'I think . . .' Duke paused and thought. 'I think they only put up with him because he was a worker and good with plants. I mean, when he put something in, you knew it'd grow. Just like with yourself, Miss. But they never did have the time of day for him, not to chat or anything.'

'Not Miss Janet?'

'Especially not Miss Janet. She wasn't above helping in the garden, now and again, she enjoyed it, but she'd ask what needed doing and then get out of his way.'

'And you never noticed anything . . . odd?'

'I don't know what you mean.'

This was hardly surprising, because May herself had very little idea what she meant, but having risked under-cutting Will Largs's interrogation of Jim Ferrier she felt a need to make amends. She decided on one last question. 'So nobody did anything that sticks in your mind as having been not the sort of thing they'd usually do?'

Duke pondered some more. 'Not at the time you're talking about,' he said. 'But later, after they'd both gone away, I saw one funny thing. Mr Mellor started jogging. Just a day or two before he died, I saw him jogging round the garden. He wasn't going anywhere special, just running round the paths. I looked to see if something was chasing him, but there wasn't. It stuck in my mind, like you said, because he was an old man and his colour was bad.'

'Yes,' May said. 'That's weird all right. Did anything else strike you as weird?'

'Can't say that it did.'

Duke was reliable and conscientious, May thought, but nobody would ever accuse him of being the brightest fairy light on the Christmas tree. She was running short of meaningful questions. Surely if the boy had seen somebody burying a body he would have said so. 'Did you see who planted that *sequoia*?' she asked.

'That what?'

'The conifer that used to be in that bed near where you stopped the mower.'

'Oh that. That was Charlie Mostyn. I'd left my jacket in the shed one day and when I went back for it I saw him putting it in.'

Ten

May would have had plenty to occupy her hands in the garden but for once she ignored the call. There was too much occupying her mind.

She went indoors and spent some time with her photographs. She paced restlessly around for a few minutes, her mind full of unwelcome thoughts, and then walked to the Lodge. In the temporary Incident Room she found only a civilian clerk sorting papers. Superintendent Largs and Inspector Welles had gone back to Inverness for a conference. Beyond that, if he knew anything, he was not prepared to divulge it. May returned to her cottage and went to the phone.

Will Largs, she was told, had gone out but she was put through to Bob Welles's extension. While she waited, she thought that she heard a car, but the beat was definitely not that of the big four-by-four. She was distracted from it by Bob's voice as he came on the line. 'Did you ever compare the spectacle lens you found with Joe Scott's body with the prescription of Charles Mostyn at Craigwells Farm?' she asked him.

'Off the top of the head, I can't tell you. Probably not, if he didn't get his prescription filled locally. His name hasn't figured in the case. I'll check.'

The sitting room darkened. May thought that a black cloud must have covered the sky but when she glanced round she saw that the day beyond the window remained bright. Light falling through the open front door had been reflecting off the white wall of the passage until the figure of an enormously large woman, taller than May and several times her weight, blocked it out. From her several chins and her pumpkin-like breasts, rolls of fat descended to the woman's ankles which overflowed her shoes. Incongruously, the caricature figure was surmounted by tight, blonde curls and a face beginning to sag but once of almost angelic prettiness. She wore a loose smock. Any other form of clothing would have been impractical.

May was almost sure that there had been no knock, but she remained polite. 'Can I help you?' she asked.

'Aye, likely,' the woman said. 'You're the wumman wha found Joey Scott's corp?' Her accent, May thought, was Aberdeen – and not from one of the better areas. To May it suggested the fish market and indeed a faint smell of fresh haddock seemed to follow as she squeezed into the sitting room.

'That's right,' May said.

'Weel, I'm his weedow. I seen the polis and I got the wee bit of his gear they haid and his Post Office bookie. Whaur's the rest o't?'

'I don't know about anything else,' May said. 'His clothes, even his spares, and his toilet things seem to have been buried with him. I gave the police anything that I found here that didn't go with the house.'

'Is that so?' The woman pushed further into the cottage. Her attitude was definitely menacing. May became aware that her mouth had dried. 'Is that right?' the woman resumed in tones of disbelief. 'There's naethin o' his in here?'

'Not a damn thing,' May said. 'There's some furniture in one of the sheds but it's only fit for firewood.'

179

'He wrat me he wis gaunae sen me his guid watch.' Her eyes fastened on May's wrist. 'Hey, is that it?'

May was losing patience. 'No it is bloody well not,' she said. 'Get out of here.'

The woman lumbered towards her and reached for her wrist. 'Gimme ma Joey's watch.'

The watch on May's wrist looked good but it was a cheap copy in a gilt case. If the woman had asked for it as a favour May would almost certainly have given it to her. But the manner of asking made it impossible to accede. 'Go to hell,' May said and as the other came within reach she gave her a push in the monstrous chest.

She might as well have pushed against a haystack or a sack of frogspawn. Her hands seemed to sink in but the mass never gave an inch. The push seemed to infuriate the woman. She gave May a push in return which sent her staggering back against the sitting-room wall and followed up, using sheer bulk to pin May against the wall while grabbing for May's wrist. A small table went over with the sound of ornaments smashing.

May's temper went and she experienced a spasm of rage such as she had not known since her early childhood. The large, soft body was smothering her movements, but the two heads were close. She headbutted. Her brow struck the other over the mouth. The jolt induced a flash of light inside May's head but the adrenaline rush anaesthetized pain. The other woman jerked back and May, her hands now free, followed up instinctively and, cupping the two vast and unrestrained breasts, banged them together with all her might.

Mrs Scott – if she was truly entitled to the name – was hurt. Blood was spreading over the lower part of her face. But she was roused to new fury and produced a roundhouse punch which sent May staggering against the fire-place. Her clock went down into the hearth. Following up, the woman caught May by the hair. A single lock would have torn out, but not the whole scalp. Discounting the pain as irrelevant for the moment, May caught the wo-man's other wrist before she could give more than one jab to May's face. The other was strong, but years of garden-ing had hardened May's muscles. One hand was enough. May's other hand was free. She clawed at the woman's face, feeling for eyes to poke, nose to twist, anything to relieve the cumulating agony of her hair.

Somehow it worked, though moments later May came to feel that it had been a case of out of the frying pan into the fire. The grip on her hair was released for a moment but shifted to her throat as she was pushed back against the wall.

May was in serious trouble. Consciousness would not last long. The world was turning grey. She knew momen-tary relief to the sound of a furious growling, which she thought came from the other woman. But the growling came from Ellery who had followed up the sounds of strife and, with the instinctive need to protect her mistress overriding the spaniel's naturally soft mouth, had launched an attack on the big woman's flabby buttocks.

The relief did not last. The woman's rage combined with the protection of layers of insensitive fat, enabled her to ignore the assault except for a back-heel which made the spaniel utter a muffled yelp. Ellery hung on, swinging like a pendulum from a fold of flesh, and then, caught by a second back-heel, let go.

May was close to blacking out. In desperation, she flung out her free hand and found, on the mantelpiece, her one unbroken ornament, a soapstone figure that her father had brought back from a visit to Hong Kong. In a single movement she snatched it up, balanced its weight and caught the other woman a glancing blow across the head. The grip slackened enough to allow her a deep breath. She swung again, a stronger and better-aimed blow, which caught the other above the ear. The woman released her grip and staggered three precious paces back, knocking over the coffee table. Her mouth was swelling fast, she had lost at least two teeth and blood from her nose was dripping on to May's carpet. There was more blood seeping into the blonde curls. But her rage was undimmed. There was a red glint in her eyes. She moved forward again, her hands hooked into talons.

Ellery was afraid but her fear was for her mistress. Barking, she charged in again only to be bowled over by a kick that sent her into the corner of the room.

May's fury was at least a match, outstripping her earlier anger tenfold. Her room, her refuge against a cruel world, was wrecked, her precious ornaments were broken and the mountainous harpy was coming in again. Her beloved spaniel, dependent on her for care and protection, had been assaulted. (The fact that Ellery had first assaulted the woman somehow escaped May's attention.) Ellery had recovered her breath and was circling, barking loudly but preparing to rush in again. Another such kick might well do permanent damage. May raised the soapstone carving, determined to splash the other's brains over the walls and ceiling. Her life was too precious to risk in a renewed battle against overwhelming weight and padding.

There came an intervention for which May was to be eternally grateful. A male figure pushed between them and thrust them apart, holding each by the hair. May's scalp was already tender from the earlier tugging, but through her tears she managed to recognize Charlie Mostyn, the farmer. His reach was longer than that of either woman, rendering him comparatively safe. Rage began to drain out of May, allowing pain to take its place. Her hair was released and she found herself pushed backwards into one of the easy chairs. The soapstone figure was detached from her hand and replaced gently on the mantel. The big woman was pushed back to the doorway. Ellery, aware that the battle was over, retired behind the couch.

Mrs Scott, meanwhile, from seething, was also beginning to cool. Tears of pain and self-pity dimmed the glaring eyes. 'I'll hae the laa on ye,' she said. 'You dug's a savage baist. I'll hae it pit doon. I ken my rights.'

She turned and lumbered out of the room. May began to rise but Charlie checked her. 'When somebody says that,' he remarked, 'they usually don't. Let her go, for God's sake. What the hell were you fighting about with Joe's widow?'

From outside came the sound of a car, roughly treated, driving away. May ducked under Charlie's arm and went to the window. An ancient saloon was disappearing from sight, leaning heavily to the right like a man carrying a suitcase full of books.

May drew deep breaths through her mouth. Her nose seemed to be blocked. She was shaking and she thought that she might be going to cry. She tried to speak but her throat was too painful. She led the way into her kitchen and took a chilled bottle of milk from the refrigerator. The cold milk eased and lubricated her throat. 'She wanted Joe's watch,' she said hoarsely. Her blood was up and her usual irresolution was in abeyance. 'It's all right, I didn't tell her that you'd got it. She won't be coming back for you.'

Charlie lowered his arm so that his sleeve slipped over the watch. 'I don't know what you mean,' he said.

'I think you do. In fact, I'm damn sure of it. Charlie, you killed Joe, didn't you? I can't say that I blame you, but, honest to God, you can't let Jim Ferrier go to jail for it. Did you kill Janet as well?'

Instead of an answer, Charlie drew May to the sink. He filled a basin with cold water, added ice cubes from the refrigerator and, while she began the process of repairing her face, fetched her flannel from the bathroom. She stole a glance into the small mirror on one of the shelves and recoiled. Her face looked like a filmmaker's vision for a video nasty and it would be worse before it was better. Her forehead was visibly swelling but at least her nose seemed to be unbroken.

'Are there any more ice cubes?' she asked. Her voice was coming a little more easily.

'That was the last of them.'

'There's a bag of frozen peas in the freezer. They've gone long past their use-by date. Drop the whole bag in here, please.'

The icy water was helping to slow the development of the bruises and it seemed to have stopped both her nose-bleed and her desire to explode into tears. She put her whole face into the water for as long as she could hold her breath and then resorted to dabbing again.

'No, I didn't kill either of them,' Charlie said from behind her. 'If you really thought I had, you must have been out of your bloody mind to say what you did and then hang your head over a basin of water while we're alone here, don't you think? I could have drowned you like a puppy.'

'I was too grateful for being saved from that harridan,' May said. 'I felt . . . Oh, never mind what I felt. What brought you here anyway?' She put her face down into the water again.

'I've got your load of dung outside. I just wanted to know if you wanted it tipped in the usual place. Are you hearing me?'

Without lifting her face, May raised a thumb.

She heard Charlie take a deep breath. 'I don't want you running around with that mad idea,' he said, 'so I suppose I'd better tell you what really happened. Can you still hear me?' Again May held up a thumb in reply. 'Right, then. The day Joe . . . vanished. It was a Sunday. I'm not a keeper of the Sabbath but I don't go out of my way to let folk see me breaking it. That makes it a good day for odd jobs. Joe had had eelworm in his potatoes and the ground wasn't clear of it for planting tatties again yet, so Mr Mellor had ordered two sacks from me and I could bring them in the boot of the car without offending anybody.

'I came down the drive towards the back door and saw Mr Mellor standing outside the tool shed with Joe lying at his feet.'

May had been raising her face intermittently to snatch occasional breaths, but now she gasped without first taking her face out of the water. She coughed and choked herself to a standstill and made a wordless sound of interrogation.

'Oh, it's true,' Charlie said. 'He was in a hell of a state, in the middle of an angina attack. He begged me to help him and I was fond of the old gentleman. Frankly, he was a better man than any ten others around here and he'd been a big help to me, in a business way, when my dad was in his final illness and I had to come back quick and take over.

185

So I agreed. Of course I did. First I got his spray out of his pocket and sprayed it under his tongue. I know about bad hearts – that's how my dad went.

'As I said, it was Sunday, so the staff were off. Mrs Mellor had gone with Colin Wilson to visit her sister-in-law.

'I wanted to help the old chap. All the same, I wasn't going to have Joe on my land. I never could thole that man. I dug a hole in the nearest bed, all the time expecting somebody to come up the drive but they never did. While I dug, Mr Mellor went to this cottage. We got rid of enough of his clothes and things along with the body to make it look as if Joe had gone off of his own accord. And Mr Mellor showed me the small tree and we put it in above the body. We thought the tree would be there for a hundred years, and by then nobody would give much of a damn about Joe.'

May raised her head and took several deep breaths. 'And you broke your spectacles. I noticed from my photographs that your new ones date from the same time.'

'I was sweating. They slid off my nose just as I dug the spade in. I picked up all the bits but my vision was blurred and there was one lens I couldn't find. Up to then, Mr Mellor had only given me the barest gist of the story, but when all was done we came in here to the bathroom to clean up, so as to leave no traces in the house. Mr Mellor's spray had done the trick by then and his angina was almost gone. I made a cup of tea and we sat down and he gave me the rest of the tale.

'He'd decided to cut some flowers, to please Mrs Mellor when she came back. Funny how these small decisions can turn out. He headed for the tool shed to find a pair of secateurs and met Joe, who was on his way out, dressed up, to catch the bus and meet some woman. He usually had a tatty old pocket watch but he must have taken out the good watch to impress his fancy woman. They stopped to have a word and Mr Mellor noticed the watch on Joe's wrist.'

May's face had had as much icy water as it could stand. She turned to face Charlie while she dabbed her face very gently with paper towels. Thought was an effort. 'You mean Janet's watch. It was a present from Mr Mellor on her eighteenth birthday. She shows up wearing it in some of my photographs of the garden and so do you. The other thing I've just noticed is that, until the time of Joe's disappearance, you were wearing a silver digital.'

Ellery had ventured out from behind the sitting-room sofa and she came to nose May's hand, uncertain whether her attack on the big woman had been a mistaken reaction to some friendly game or a justifiable defence of her mistress. May knelt down to reassure the spaniel, but keeping her face well out of reach of the roving tongue. A lick might be well intentioned but it would be less than hygienic.

Charlie leaned back against the door of May's broom cupboard. He looked drained. 'That's what it was all about. Until then, the Mellors had been hoping that Janet had gone off with a boyfriend. Seeing her watch on Joe's wrist put a different complexion on it.' Charlie glanced down at his own wrist. 'When we'd finished, Mr Mellor said that I'd better have the watch. It was all he could do for me in the way of thankyou. Is it really special? I took it for one of those fakes.'

'It cost a packet,' May said. 'There are fakes of that model, but you can tell the difference. The movement of the second hand gives them away. Go on.'

'Well, that's about it. Mr Mellor taxed Joe with stealing

the watch and with doing away with Janet. Joe had been drinking – I could smell whisky on his corpse. He blustered and denied it and Mr Mellor kept tripping him up until Joe suddenly cracked and blurted out his side of the story. Mr Mellor was crying as he told me this.

'Joe had made a pass at Janet when she was doing a little work in the garden. That had been another time when he'd been on the booze. She was furious. She was going to get him sacked and she also knew about him growing cannabis and was going to tell the police. Joe lost his rag and snatched up the garden fork. Say what you will about Joe, he always kept his tools sharp. When he realized what he'd done, he put her behind the wall and buried her where the roses were going to go.

'When Joe admitted as much to Janet's father, Mr Mellor saw red and hit him with the hatchet.'

Silence fell, a vacuum. The subject was exhausted except for things better left unexplored. May got to her feet, looked in the mirror again and was not comforted. As a small step in the right direction, she tried to tidy her hair. Her body was enveloped in lassitude but she found that her mind was working freely again.

'I suppose it'll all come out now,' Charlie said.

'I think it must. I've already mentioned the spectacle lens to the police. Duke Ellon saw you plant the tree, although he's as thick as glue and he hasn't seen the significance of it yet.' May found that her new mood of determination was still in charge. 'I think you'd better get out of here. Leave the watch with me, if you like, and don't make any statement to the police until we've spoken again. I'll do what I can. And, Charlie, thanks again for galloping to the rescue. I couldn't have been happier to see the whole US Cavalry. I'll do the same for you, some day.'

Eleven

Charlie Mostyn was more concerned over May's injuries than about his own invidious position. May had to lead him to his tractor before he would accept that she was recovered enough to be left alone. He left at last to deposit his dung in 'the usual place' behind the walled garden. May paid for the dung, just to get rid of his motherly presence, and made a note to claim recompense from Grant Wheatley.

Janet Mellor's watch she put in her favourite hiding place behind the chest of drawers. Whatever she decided to do with it, she did not want the police to set eyes on it until she had thought it over. She wondered whether to start sorting out the sitting room or repairing the damage to her appearance, but her head was ringing and she was emotionally at her limit. She decided that both tasks were beyond her capability, took two paracetamols and lay down on her bed.

She must have slept because, although it seemed only a few minutes later, her bedside clock had made a big jump forward when she was roused by a rapping at her door. Her face was very tender and all her muscles were so stiff that she moved like a very old woman. A glance in the mirror assured her that she looked worse than she felt. The rapping was repeated. She called that she was coming and passed a hasty brush over her hair. Better, but a drop in the ocean.

She tried to open the door no more than a crack. Will Largs was on the doorstep. 'You can't come in,' she said.

'Are you not decent?' He sounded amused, perhaps a little intrigued.

An affirmative answer would only have persuaded him to wait. 'It's not that,' she said. 'It's a bad time. Please go away.'

Her voice gave her away. 'Something's wrong. What is it?' Will asked sharply. He waited for a few seconds and then said, 'I'm not going away, so you may as well let me in.'

His tone was not that of a forceful policeman but of a concerned friend and she felt comforted immediately. 'Come in if you must,' she said, 'but don't look at me.'

As she spoke, she knew that the command was impossible. As soon as she opened the door, he pulled her towards the daylight. 'My God!' he said. 'Who did this to you? I'll tear him in half.'

His tone was so indignant that she was instantly cheered. She nearly laughed, but that would have hurt her face too much. Instead, she sighed. 'You can't, you're a policeman. You're not supposed to go around tearing people in half until after they've been cautioned and charged. And this one would take more tearing than even you could manage. You'd better come all the way inside.' Without conscious decision, she leaned against him and he put an arm round her. His sympathy stole away her strength. She kept her head down to hide the tears, which had come at last, but he put his hand under her chin and lifted her face.

'Do you need medical attention?' he asked.

She almost smiled again to see the policeman taking

over. 'I don't think so,' she said huskily. 'There are no bones broken and no cuts. I should mend in my own time.'

He looked into her eyes and seemed satisfied. May told herself that he was only looking for signs of concussion. He steered her to the sitting-room door. She nearly said, 'Not in here,' but there was nowhere else. He gave the room one embracing glance and then lowered her on to the couch. He stepped carefully over the litter on the floor to the window, closed the curtains and returned, fragments of china crunching underfoot. His voice came gently out of the dimness. 'Now you don't have to see it,' he said.

'And you don't have to look at me.'

'There is that. Just sit quietly for a minute.'

He left the room and she heard voices outside. He returned, joined her on the couch and put his arm round her again. 'Bob Welles was to join me here but I've sent him back to base. I can phone for a car when I'm ready to go. Tell me what happened.'

'Joe Scott's widow happened.'

'That gorgon!' he exclaimed.

'You've met the lady? I don't think you could tear her in half, in fact it might go the other way around. She seemed to think that I was keeping some of Joe's valuables here. I told her to go away and we started pushing each other.' May gathered the rags of her courage to make her confession. 'It turned into a real fight, no holds barred. I think the Americans call it knock-down-and-drag-out. We both lost our tempers but she's bigger than I am. If Charlie Mostyn hadn't turned up, I think one of us would have killed the other. And I'd got my hands on that soapstone figure of Confucius, or whoever it is, so you'd probably be charging me with something terminal. He pulled us apart,

191

sent her away and stood by while I soaked my bruises in ice water and fought off the hysterics.'

'Mostyn the farmer? Good for him. He must be a brave man,' Will said grimly. 'We had her at the station earlier this morning. She seemed quite convinced that the evil police had embezzled her Joey's cash and treasures. She was quite prepared to fight the lot of us and you're right, it would take the whole of the Highland Constabulary working together to tear her in half. Do you want to prosecute?'

That was a new thought. May managed a shaky laugh while keeping her face straight. 'I wouldn't want the police going into danger on my account. What brings you here?'

'Bob Welles told me that the spectacle lens matched the prescription of your rescuer. I wanted to come out here with Bob anyway, so I decided to call and ask you to tell me all about how you knew.'

'I didn't really know, I made a guess, but I know now. I'll tell you about it in a minute. What's happening about Jim Ferrier?'

She felt him shrug. 'We've let him go. This is the damnedest case. It's like running in treacle – down the garden path, you might say. Nothing fits together and nobody wants to tell us anything relevant. I'm not convinced that he's innocent but we've nothing like enough to hold him on. It's all motive; and motive never made a case.'

'He *is* innocent,' May said. 'Facts have been almost throwing themselves at me. I can hand you the whole thing on a plate. But first I want you to promise me two things. About Charlie Mostyn. First, remember that if it hadn't been for him I might have been killed or else be in serious trouble for killing Mrs Scott. Honest to God, it was as bad as that.'

'I shan't forget it,' Will said.

'The second follows on. I'll come back to it later. First I'd better give you the facts.'

'Is this going to be a long story?'

'I think it may be.'

'Then I know what you need. But first . . .' He took out a very white handkerchief and dried her cheeks before giving her a gentle kiss below each eye. He got up and set the coffee table on its legs. It seemed to be unbroken.

He went through to her kitchen and she sat, stupefied but trying to clear her thoughts and to pretend that her aches and pains were happening to somebody else. Her eyes had adjusted to the dim light filtering through the curtains so she closed them against the sight of her ruined room. She heard him making tea.

His eyes had lost their adjustment to the darkness. When he came back with a tray bearing two steaming mugs and a plate of biscuits, she had to take it from him, put it on the table and guide him to his seat beside her.

'How's that?' he asked.

'You must have had a lot of practice, coddling witnesses. And suspects.'

'I have staff to do all that. When you're ready.'

Between nibbles at biscuits and sips of the best tea ever infused, May embarked on her story. 'I'll tell you later who to go to for evidence,' she said. 'For the moment, here are the bones of what I've found out. Joe Scott killed Janet. His motives are blurred, which isn't surprising because he seems to have been drunk at the time, but a mixture of a rejected pass and a threat to get him fired for that or prosecuted for growing cannabis would have added up to quite enough. I met Joe once or twice when he'd been on the drink. He was one of your aggressive, cantankerous drunks.'

'Not like you, in fact.' She felt him shake with a chuckle, quickly past.

'Not at all like me. I get sloppy and affectionate. But don't get your hopes up, it doesn't often happen.' May paused to collect her thoughts. 'He put her behind the drystone wall and started the dumping of soil on top of her. But he kept her watch. It's a very expensive one, rather large for a lady's wristwatch, quite masculine-looking in fact because she was long-sighted and her near vision was never very good. Joe promised the watch to his wife. They were separated but still good friends – but you probably know all about that. Meantime, he wore it when he was going out looking for sex. He wouldn't have dared to wear it when the Mellors were around. You can track it from person to person in my photographs.

'On one occasion when Joe was setting off to meet some woman, Mrs Mellor had gone visiting. Joe probably thought that Mr Mellor had gone with her, but I remember that Mr Mellor couldn't stick his wife's brother at any price. Mr Mellor bumped into Joe unexpectedly by the tool shed. He recognized the watch and accused Joe. Joe had been drinking again. He blustered a bit but in the end he admitted it. There was an explosive row and Mr Mellor gave Joe a whack with the hatchet.'

So far, May had adhered strictly to the truth, but the time had arrived for what she thought of as a modest adaptation. 'Mr Mellor set about burying the body. Remember, he was an elderly man with a heart condition. Charlie Mostyn, the farmer, arrived to deliver two sacks of potatoes and found him in a collapsed state. Mr Mellor was a good man and Charlie was in his debt – morally, not financially. Mr Mellor begged for Charlie's help, so Charlie finished the filling-in and planted the tree for him. Mr

Mellor insisted that Charlie keep the watch – not as a bribe but as a gift of gratitude and, I rather suspect, because he preferred Mrs Mellor to go on believing that Janet had left of her own accord. Sight of the watch would have given the game away.'

'No doubt about that,' Will said slowly. 'And this explains why your farmer friend was so determined not to pull the tree out again.'

'Exactly. Charlie was unhappy about his position but even less happy about the prospect of betraying his friend and benefactor. He was still hesitating over what to do when Mr Mellor died. I think – but perhaps you don't want my guesses?'

Will gave her shoulder a pat. 'Your guesses have been right on target so far. Let's have more of them.'

'Very well. Mr Mellor must have decided that he couldn't tell any of the story without telling it all. He decided to leave Janet buried where she was, among the roses. I noticed that he seemed to take a special interest in the roses. He had always enjoyed the garden, to sit in or stroll round smelling the flowers, but he never worked in it, he left that to his wife until near the end. Then he started paying attention to that one bed, pruning and spraying and raking over. I think that it was his way of tending his daughter's grave.

'You can imagine how he felt. He couldn't give Janet a proper burial without breaking his wife's heart and provoking an awful scandal. But he never was a very religious man and perhaps he felt that a resting place among the roses had something to commend it. The guilt he could do nothing about.

'Soon afterwards, Mr Mellor was seen jogging round the garden when he thought nobody could see him. An elderly man with a serious heart condition. My guess is that, between grief and remorse, he felt that it was time to go. He had a damaged heart so his days were numbered anyway, and on top of that he'd lost his daughter. He also wanted to spare Mrs Mellor any risk of his being prosecuted and leave her with the belief that Janet might some day come back. Inducing a fatal heart attack was his way of committing suicide without a scandal. Charlie decided to honour his wishes. There was nothing to be gained and a lot to be lost by dragging it all into the open.'

Will Largs brooded in silence for several minutes while absently stroking May's shoulder. She could see his face clearly in the dimness and she understood why some of his friends had referred to him as 'ogreish'. 'It certainly hangs together,' he said at last. 'But what evidence is there to support it?'

May braced herself. 'I said that I'd tell you the witnesses,' she said, 'and I will. But the vital witness is Charlie Mostyn. He had the whole story direct from Mr Mellor, but he'd be mad to tell it in court, or even to you, if you're going to use his statement to prosecute him for complicity or being an accessory or something.'

'There's no such offence in Scotland as being an accessory. The charge would have to be attempting to pervert the course of justice, or some such wording.'

'That sounds even worse. Will, listen to me,' May said earnestly. 'I'd be quite in the wrong to ask you for favours or to try to put any pressure on you. So I'm telling you up front that, though I had the story from him, I'm not going to repeat it. Mine would only be hearsay anyway.'

She felt Will stiffen. She thought that he was going to remove his arm, but he kept his grip on her. 'Unless I go easy on him? And you think that that's not putting pressure on me? You know that I can't do that, not even for your sake.'

May drew courage from his mild tone and from the fact that he had not pushed her away. 'That isn't what I said and you know it. I'm not asking you to do it for my sake,' she said. 'That would be quite wrong. But Charlie's a good man and he got pitchforked into an impossible situation. He kept silent for the sake of his friend and then for his friend's widow.' May decided that truth, always an elastic commodity, might stretch a little further. 'He was trying to make up his mind to come to you when I heard that he had been seen planting the tree. Then I spotted the watch and I dragged the story out of him.'

'And you're asking me to let up on him?'

'I'm not asking you anything. Perhaps I'm suggesting it.'

'All right. Then I'm asking you, just as a matter of curiosity, what you would have liked me to do if the law would allow it.'

May thought that he was probably laughing at her but she decided that his question required an answer. 'I've seen you being buddy-buddies with the Procurator Fiscal,' she said. 'And you know even better than I do that there's a whole range of different things that any offence can be called. You see it all the time when cases are being reported. They talk about the charge being reduced to so-and-so or "proceeding only on the lesser charge". Attempting to pervert the course of justice would be at one end of the scale and I suppose wasting police time would be at the other. Because he saved me from becoming either a killer or a victim, I'm hoping that you'll do what you can to get Charlie off with a light sentence, or a fine and probation if that's possible.'

'And if I promise you that, you'll see that he tells the whole story?'

May swallowed. 'I'm trying not to put any extra pressure on you. If you can't or won't, I'll still be your friend if you want me to.'

There was a long silence. May thought that she could read Will's thoughts, perhaps through minute changes in the pressure of his arm. He would have the right to resent her suggestion, but she could sense friendship in his clasp and, if there was more to be divined, it was not hostility.

'If your witnesses come through, I'll do what I can,' Will said at last. 'It wouldn't even be my decision, you understand. The Procurator Fiscal would decide.'

'And you'll try to avoid a scandal? Both the killers are dead but Mrs Mellor is still alive.'

'All right. Mrs Mellor knows about the finding of Janet's body, of course, and looking back over the two interviews I had with her I rather think that she suspects at least part of the truth. I don't see anything to be gained by publicity at this late stage. But that's as far as I could possibly go and a lot further than I should. For now, I need some time to think it over. You're sure of your facts?'

'As far as they go, yes.'

'Then a few interviews with your witnesses should be enough to wind the case up. May I use your phone? I'm going to stand the team down and start again tomorrow morning with the minimum of men needed to take statements.' He suddenly kissed her cheek, clumsily, and hugged May until her sore ribs protested. 'Bless you, you've done my job for me. Will you be all right now, if I leave you alone?'

'I'll be all right,' May said slowly. It was her first downright lie. She would not be all right if he left her alone. She would be desolate. 'Hungry but all right – I seem to have slept through my mealtime. If you can bear to look at me with lumps all over my face . . .'

'I can't even see you,' Will said with amusement in his voice and May realized that daylight had been fading away while they talked.

She tried to unclench her fists. She had made enough decisive efforts for one day, but another was called for. 'What I am trying in my clumsy way to say is that you don't have to go away tonight at all if you don't want to.'

'But your bruises—?'

'You can kiss them better,' May said desperately. 'But don't if you don't want to.'

'You know that I want to, more than anything else on earth.' He turned and kissed her properly, very gently brushing her swollen lips. It was as exciting as she had known it would be. 'Did you say that you were hungry?' he said huskily. 'So am I. Lend me the keys of your Mini, then lean back and relax. The nearest carryout's only a few miles off.'

'Why is the Procurator Fiscal called a procurator fiscal?' May asked. 'I thought *fiscal* meant about money.'

'It does,' Will said. 'Originally, the post was concerned with the collecting of fines.'

In a mood of mutual satisfaction and contentment next morning, they were beginning to clear up the debris in May's sitting room. May, in particular, was congratulating herself on having found that great rarity the perfect lover – passionate but gentle, persistent yet patient. Their union had proved to be as much emotional as physical.

At the sound of footsteps, May made a dart for the door but she was too late. Polly had formed the habit of walking in without waiting to be invited. She did so now, towing

Grant in her wake. They checked at the sight of Will Largs, massive in his shirtsleeves, but were more concerned at May's appearance. Her bruises had progressed from blue-black to a variegation of colours which she might have welcomed in a flower species. 'What on earth happened to your face?' Polly asked. Her eyes flicked involuntarily towards Will and then around the shattered room. Had a lovers' tiff got out of hand?

'Joe Scott's widow happened to it,' May explained hastily. 'She went for me, but I think I gave as good as I got.' May had been reared in circles where sex before marriage was barely mentioned, let alone considered per-missible, and she cringed inwardly. She could see Polly, and then Grant, adding together the early hour, Will's presence, the post-coital aura, which undoubtedly sur-rounded them, and the absence of a car at the door. She could only offer silent thanks that they were both dressed and a prayer that the shattered state of the room was not being taken as evidence of some passionate orgy. She pushed aside an almost overwhelming desire to giggle. 'Don't blame Will,' she said. 'He isn't that much of a demon lover.'

Will Largs, as conventional in his way as May was in hers, felt impelled to rush to the aid of her reputation. 'I have asked May to marry me,' he said. That, it seemed, made it all right.

Polly and Grant expressed delight. Polly, indeed, went into the raptures proper to a successful matchmaker. May had some recollection of marriage having been mentioned during the transports of the night but she was fairly sure that no conclusion had been reached. 'I never said—' she began.

Nobody was listening.

200

'But this is splendid! You must be married from Can-naluke Lodge,' Polly said. 'Nothing could be more suit-able. We must celebrate.' She dashed outside.

May decided to try again. 'My mother could never afford—'

'But it will be my gift,' Grant said. Will began to protest but Grant rode him down. 'I insist. I've been looking into the estate records, May, and I see that your salary – wage – whatever you want to call it – hadn't been revised since the year dot. You've been grossly underpaid and all the while you've been creating an asset that will keep me in happi-ness for at least another forty years.'

'But I still haven't said—'

'I'll insist on contributing,' Will said. By the time of Polly's return with a bottle of champagne and four flutes, agreement had been reached. Will would pay for the cars, the church and the bridesmaids' dresses while Grant would be responsible for the wines and catering. May or her mother could provide the bride's dress.

'I will not have a white—'

'It's what you were afraid of, all the same,' Polly told her husband as she poured champagne. 'We lose the best gardener in the world.'

May began again. 'I have no intention—'

'It's quite simple,' Grant said. 'We take on a brace of May's school-leavers and pay her a retainer to come over every week or two and keep them straight.'

'I can't quarrel with that,' Will said. 'Frankly, you seem to have settled everything except the bridesmaids.'

'Unless May has somebody in mind . . .?' Grant began.

'No, I—'

'Then why not dispense with bridesmaids and have two matrons of honour, Polly and Jenny?'

'Love to,' Polly said. 'So will Jenny.'

'You'll have to act alone,' Grant said. 'Jenny must take the photographs.'

May gave up. She had made more than enough decisions for the moment and the outcome would probably be satisfactory. She got up and walked quietly out on a discussion of music and caterers. Outside, she whistled up Ellery. Her beloved flowers were calling, but first she went into a greenhouse and started putting aside a careful selection of young plants. She would need them when she came to reshape Will's garden in Beauly.